QUE SERA SERA

Elizabeth Neill

MINERVA PRESS
LONDON
ATLANTA MONTREUX SYDNEY

QUE SERA SERA
Copyright © Elizabeth Neill 1998

All Rights Reserved

No part of this book may be reproduced in any form,
by photocopying or by any electronic or mechanical means,
including information storage or retrieval systems,
without permission in writing from both the copyright
owner and the publisher of this book.

ISBN 1 86106 992 8

First Published 1998 by
MINERVA PRESS
195 Knightsbridge
London SW7 1RE

Printed in Great Britain for Minerva Press

QUE SERA SERA

All characters and events in this book are fictional and any resemblance to actual places, events or persons, living or dead, is purely coincidental.

*This book is dedicated to my family,
for all the love and understanding (and the confusion!)
that being a member of a family involves.*

Part One
Duncan's Story

Chapter One

Duncan was born a Yorkshireman as was his father, grandfather and great-grandfather before him. He was the middle son; his older brother was two years his senior and he had a younger brother who was eight years his junior. His mother, a very well-rounded lady, had always held a firm belief that, if she left a large gap between her middle child and the youngest, then surely a daughter would arrive on the scene! But her hopes and prayers were to no avail as yet another son appeared into her world. Somehow, for her, this third son became her most cherished and treasured of all and a deep bond grew between mother and son. Despite this, there was never any jealousy amongst the brothers and they grew up in a typically close-knit Northern family, where the father came home to lunch from the office and high tea was served promptly at five o'clock each day.

The three brothers certainly had very different characters. Graham, the eldest, was always the most serious. He did have a sense of humour, but it was not so evident as it was in the other two boys who inherited theirs from their mother, who literally shook from head to toe when she laughed. Graham had decided right from his final years at school that he wanted to pursue banking as his career. On leaving school, he applied to one of the large banks where he was duly accepted for training.

With very little thought needed, Duncan decided that surveying would be his choice and he set out to become a chartered surveyor. His father was an architect and so, by choosing the same line of business, Duncan received a great deal of moral support as well as practical help from him.

While the two older brothers pursued their future careers, their younger brother, Grant, was still way behind them at school and he had no idea at all what he might venture into eventually. To him it all seemed a long way off and he was quite content to concentrate on his lessons and sport. All three boys had attended the local grammar school and, whilst they didn't excel in any one thing, they proved to be average pupils, both academically and on the sports field and they were all good mixers. They found school life uncomplicated and pleasant and they were ready to take up the challenge of their chosen careers on leaving.

When Duncan left school, he was accepted into a local York firm of Chartered Surveyors. There he began his long years of training and studying to achieve his necessary qualifications. It was during this time that his mother, Dorothy, became ill with a severe attack of bronchitis. As she was such a large woman her ample chest seemed to fill the whole room with her constant coughing and gasping for breath, a noise which was very distressing for all around her to listen to.

Their family doctor, a Doctor Hunt, was duly summoned to their house and he examined Dorothy's chest and proceeded to prescribe the appropriate medication. Dr Hunt was a doctor in every sense of the word. He was adored by his patients and highly respected by his colleagues. He was well known for his accurate diagnoses and knowledge of the latest medical developments; thus he had saved many a patient from the surgeon's knife. His two favourite tonics were milk or champagne. He put his poor patients on milk and his wealthy ones on champagne, vowing that they were the finest tonics in the world! At Christmas time, his surgery became like an Aladdin's cave as all his grateful patients carried him their offerings of chickens, hams, turkeys, whisky and presents galore, all brought in to show how much they appreciated all the doctor continually did for them.

The year was 1930 and a doctor was as much a friend as a medical adviser.

Although it was Dorothy Dr Hunt had come to see, her middle son's future was unknowingly being planned! Casually, after one of many visits to Dorothy, the doctor inquired, 'Do either Graham or Duncan play tennis at all?'

'Duncan certainly does, but Graham is concentrating all his attention and spare time on a certain young lady called Kate, who is the daughter of a local policeman and who has clearly made up her mind that Graham is the man for her!' replied Dorothy.

Dr Hunt added, 'Then I would like to invite Duncan to come to my home next Saturday to play with my daughters, Mary and Emily. They nearly always have a weekly tennis party and are constantly looking out for new players to join in. Especially, I might add, tall, dark, good-looking young men!' The doctor laughed. He had a wicked twinkle in his eyes, to show he hadn't been slow to notice how Dorothy's two older sons had grown into fine, handsome young men!

So the invitation was given and in turn accepted on Duncan's behalf.

At the time of this first invitation, Duncan was a confident twenty year old who had reached adulthood as a pleasing, uncomplicated young man. He was about six feet tall, of slim build but certainly not lean, and had a thick mop of dark hair and dark brown eyes to set off his strong, well-defined face. He was a real bookworm and he pursued his chosen career with much enthusiasm and intensity.

He was very eager to learn and he studied each evening with the aid of endless cups of black coffee to keep him from nodding off! He also worked hard in the daytime, absorbing as much as he possibly could from the firm who were training him. Duncan knew that he had chosen the right career for himself and the studying was not at all tedious to him.

His mother told him of Dr Hunt's invitation for the following Saturday and Duncan went to bed that night wondering what the doctor's daughters would be like. In fact, he really wondered why he had been asked there in the first place and imagined that the doctor probably had two ugly daughters and that their father was desperate to find them young men! Duncan tried to remember whether he had ever met them in the past, but he could not recall any prior meeting. Nevertheless, the thoughts produced a happy note on which to drift off into the world of sleep.

Chapter Two

The drive up to 'Netherlands', the Hunts' family home was long and winding, with a mass of rose bushes on each side and dotted with the occasional azaleas. It presented itself as a most impressive driveway, the sort where you felt you must really be getting somewhere by the time you had reached the end of it. This held many mixed feelings of excitement and apprehension for Duncan, the nearer he got. A huge Victorian house sat comfortably and solidly at the end of this most impressive drive. Duncan thought that it seemed rather a dark building, in contrast with all the beautiful colours which he had seen on his way up to the house. On reflection many years later, Duncan was to regard this long driveway as his road of destiny and all of his younger life that had gone on before had merely been the nursery slopes.

Duncan parked his small car fairly near the front door, where the drive opened up to provide easy parking space for at least half a dozen cars or more. He got out of his car and walked briskly up to the solid oak front door with stone lions lying majestically on each side of it. By now he was very nervous and wondered whether the doctor himself would answer the ring on the bell or maybe the beautiful or ugly daughters would appear! In fact, neither the doctor nor his daughters answered, but a very grand-looking butler. Duncan felt at this stage that he should announce himself as

Lord 'Something or other' but the thought left him as quickly as it had formed in his mind. Instead he said, 'I'm Mr Duncan Robson, here at the invitation of Dr Hunt.'

'The reply came from the formally attired butler who didn't alter his stony expression at all! 'Yes, sir, the doctor is expecting you. Please follow me.'

Duncan's first impression was that the house was large and dark, certainly not small and cosy as was his parents' humble abode. After having walked through a lounge hall hung with tapestries, topped by a minstrel gallery and dotted with Ming vases and brass tubs intermittently placed on Chinese rugs, Duncan was shown into the lounge, where a Great Dane leapt up from beside the doctor's chair and came to see who had been let into his sanctuary. Doctor Hunt put some papers that he had been dealing with down on to his coffee table and came over to shake Duncan warmly by the hand. As he approached, Duncan was aware of this kindly man, whose knowledge of his profession and of his fellow men was evident in his confident persona. 'Welcome, Duncan. It's good of you to come and join us for tennis. Come on through into the garden and I'll introduce you to the girls and their friends.'

'Lovely. Thank you for your invitation. I've been really looking forward to today.'

The doctor led the way out through the French windows, which opened out on to a beautiful wide terrace which was strewn with tubs of scarlet, pink and white geraniums. Down the steps leading from the terrace, a brilliant sight welcomed Duncan. It consisted of bright, colourful garden umbrellas with white, wrought-iron tables and chairs which were littered with tennis rackets, glasses and jugs filled with squash. There were about seven people there, four of whom were already absorbed in a battle on the tennis court, while the remaining three were sitting around a table, happily watching the game and laughing and talking at the same time. Dr Hunt led Duncan to them and made the necessary introductions.

It transpired that both his daughters, Mary and Emily, were on court, partnered by two rather lean young men. However, the game being played looked fairly good without being played too seriously. As soon as Duncan saw Mary he could not wait to meet her; it was the first time in his life that he had felt so excited about meeting someone and he hoped he would not be disappointed! Mary was tall, very fair-skinned, with thick, golden hair, which Duncan was immediately very aware of, due to the way in which the sun was highlighting the tones in it. As he was gazing at her, Mary in turn noticed Duncan standing intently watching her. Realising her sudden distraction from the game, Emily called out to her sister, 'Are you ready for me to serve?'

Mary was suddenly jolted back into the game and called out a hurried 'yes.'

Emily was rather the opposite to Mary, short, also fair, but she wore thick-rimmed glasses; she seemed full of life. At last, after what seemed an endless game, Mary came off the court and walked straight up to Duncan with a warm smile and an outstretched hand.

'Hello, Duncan, I'm so glad you could come to join us and we have all been looking forward to meeting you.'

'Yes, the feeling is mutual. I am very keen to join in and only hope that my game will be up to your standard.'

Before having time to really get into deep conversation, Duncan was whisked on to the court with the other three friends, who had been watching the previous match, and he soon found himself concentrating on the matter in hand.

Meanwhile, he was very conscious of a pair of penetrating blue eyes watching his every move and this made Duncan play better than he had ever played before! When his match came to an end, he made his way to one of the tables and drank a cold refreshing drink – certainly well earned, he felt! Mary immediately drew over and sat beside him and chatted easily and happily with him.

The afternoon slipped by all too quickly and Duncan thought it was time he should be taking his leave of this delightful family. By now he was only too clear about his feelings for Mary and, when he said goodbye, he made it obvious that he would like to visit her again.

Duncan turned to Mary and said, 'It's about time I went home now, but I would first like to say goodbye to your father and thank him for the opportunity of letting me join in this afternoon.'

Mary replied, 'Right then, follow me. My father will probably be in his study by now, preparing for his week ahead.'

She led Duncan through the house to a door which opened into the doctor's study, and knocked softly as she pushed open the door.

'Daddy, sorry to interrupt, but Duncan is leaving and wishes to say goodbye before he goes.'

'Come on in both of you. Did you enjoy your tennis, young man?'

Duncan felt a sudden bond with Dr Hunt as he was addressing them as a couple; this made Duncan feel special. He glanced over at Mary and noticed that it had had a similar effect on her.

Duncan answered, 'A great afternoon, thank you, Dr Hunt, and I can safely say we all thoroughly enjoyed ourselves.'

'I am very glad to hear it and hope we will see you again soon.'

Mary added, 'That's fine by me,' and with that, she turned and smiled warmly at Duncan, who returned her gesture. Then, Mary showed Duncan to the front door and saw him to his car.

Driving home, he could not believe the speed at which love had actually struck! As he was making his way, Duncan could not help thinking that, although he had been out with other girls in the past, Mary had made a profound impact on him both mentally and physically, one which he had never experienced before.

He even took two wrong turnings on his journey home and could not sleep that night for thinking about her. Duncan made a decision, there and then, that, if Mary would have him, he was hers!

Chapter Three

The next few months became a whirl of anticipation and excitement for Duncan. He now realised how Graham's life had become so absorbed with the pursuit of Kate or Kate's pursuit of Graham! When the phone rang he was disappointed to answer it only to hear Kate's voice on the other end, but at times it did turn out to be Mary's happy, vibrant voice and, oh, how his heartbeat hastened at the sound of it! Despite his feelings towards Mary, Duncan still stuck more determinedly than ever to his studies. Now he felt there was more purpose than ever in achieving his goals – he would be a brilliant surveyor and he would one day make Mary extremely proud of him.

At this particular stage in his life, he was in no position to ask Mary to marry him. It would still be a few years before he was qualified, but he really saw no reason why he should not become engaged to her, that was providing she would accept him! Their courtship steered a steady and happy course. Duncan was convinced that Mary was the girl for him and could not even imagine that another female could ever compete for the deep feelings that he held for her. Mary had also fallen for him in a big way, with his good looks and equally good manners; she was also sure that she had made the right choice from the numerous suitors she had had as she grew older. She appreciated all the studies he still had to do and was quite happy to see him only twice a week. Saturday became their weekly ritual and in the summer Duncan was invited up to 'Netherlands' for tennis and it usually ended up with a meal in the evening and sometimes a dance. The two of them made a very handsome couple, Duncan being dark and tall, Mary blonde and of a compatible height; they proved a popular couple and were invited to many local parties and also out to dinner. As Mary's father was a doctor, he was very well known in the surrounding districts and most of his patients took an interest in his beloved elder daughter's romance. It certainly gave them something else to talk about with their doctor besides their ailments, and Dr Hunt never tired of giving the latest progress report on Mary and Duncan's relationship.

The young couple decided eventually, after a year's courtship, to announce their engagement and a huge party was given for them at 'Netherlands'. Nothing was spared in giving Duncan and Mary an evening to remember – a dance band arrived, caterers moved in and the champagne flowed. It was a beautiful evening with Duncan making a short speech of thanks to Dr Hunt and his wife for their blessings on his and Mary's proposed union. Their engagement was, in reality, drawn out to about three years, but they were content and both saved fervently for their future life together.

The doctor had bought them a plot of land in Knaresborough and was having a house built for them as his very generous wedding present. This rather overshadowed what present Duncan's father could give them, as his own means were nowhere near as great as the doctors. Nevertheless, James and Dorothy decided to give them the carpets and curtains for their new home and the young couple were very happy to accept the offer. Neither of them at this stage could imagine what the future held in store for them. Their life seemed well planned, happy and secure.

Their wedding day was spectacular, held in the first week of April. Because of Dr Hunt's obvious importance in the community, the marriage between Mary and Duncan became an important social event, attracting the press and numerous well-wishers, all lining up to wish them future happiness. They were married at Roundhay Parish Church, with all the necessary trimmings that money could buy, and the wedding was attended by their relatives and friends.

The reception was held at The Mansion House in Roundhay Park, in order to accommodate the seemingly endless stream of guests. Mary and Duncan had never experienced such happiness in their lives as they did that day. A honeymoon followed in the Lake District, where they enjoyed a fortnight full of fun and laughter, where they also played a great deal of golf, both of them being competent players. The Lake District provided them with good weather and happy memories of their first union together, in which Duncan showed his young bride both gentleness and respect, a feature that many people noticed in the early years of the couple's married life. At this stage, Duncan could see no further than tomorrow and he adored Mary with all his heart.

On arriving home, they had all the thrills of settling into their new house, a Tudor-style home complete with a garden going down to the River Nidd.

Mary and Duncan soon settled down to a comfortable domestic routine and proved to be great friends as well as man and wife. 'They grew to be popular with their neighbours and friends, and were well loved by their devoted families.

The first three years passed very happily without any dramas, and at the end of this time, which they jointly agreed they would need to themselves, it was wonderful when they made the announcement to everyone that their first baby was on its way. After a trouble-free pregnancy, Louise Mary was born on 22nd September, 1937, weighing six pounds five ounces and looking every inch a typical Robson, with her dark hair, round face and snub nose, which Dr Hunt always referred to as 'a little piece of putty, stuck on as an afterthought!' The rest of the family were naturally delighted with the new arrival, especially Duncan's mother, Dorothy, as her granddaughter was the first girl to be born into the Robson family for many years. Graham and Kate had also got married by this time, but their first child had turned out to be yet another Robson heir! The birth of Louise was met inevitably with even more rejoicing and happiness. Dr and Mrs Hunt were of course equally overjoyed as Louise was their first grandchild. Duncan and Mary were very quick to deal with everything that parenthood held in store for them and soon became loving and devoted parents, each sharing in the joy of watching their daughter grow and progress with every new development.

Chapter Four

After another three years of happy marriage, another daughter was born to the younger Robsons. This event was to mark the first tragedy that Mary and Duncan were to experience. They proudly had their daughter christened, Julie May, and she really was a beautiful child, with blonde hair and blue eyes. She was a Hunt through and through! She was a contented baby and well loved and looked after. Louise loved having a baby sister and, although she was only three years old, she made herself as helpful as it was possible at her tender age. Louise had never liked playing with dolls, but here was the real thing!

One night, after being bathed and fed, Julie was put to bed in her nursery and lovingly tucked down for her night's sleep. Then, at about ten o'clock, Mary had an overwhelming desire to go to her daughter.

'I will just go and see if Julie is all right,' she said to Duncan. 'I have this strong feeling that something is wrong with her.'

Duncan replied, 'She will be fine, darling, but go and put your mind at rest.'

In the nursery a terrible sight awaited Mary. Julie was lying on her back in her cot and fighting for her breath. Mary rushed to the cot and lifted her up and went downstairs with her.

'Duncan, quickly phone for my father and get him to

come over. Julie can hardly breathe.'

Dr Hunt arrived within a very short time of receiving Duncan's call. He was accompanied by a paediatrician whom he had collected *en route*, but unfortunately, it all proved to be too late. Mary and Duncan's beloved baby daughter died in Mary's arms, despite every effort to revive her little body. She had been put down for her night's sleep only five hours previously and now all her life had ebbed away from her.

Duncan and Mary suffered endless pain as a result of their younger child's death and at times Mary found it difficult to accept that life could ever return to normal. During the times that followed Julie's death, Mary's love and devotion deepened for Louise and she could hardly bear to let the little girl out of her sight. However, Mary still needed to go into a nursing home on her father's insistence, in order to recover from the shock of losing Julie. The shock was made all the worse, because there had been no illness and no warning that anything was wrong with the poor little girl.

Whilst Mary was in the nursing home, she was well looked after by a pretty, young Catholic nurse, who gave Mary endless comfort and reassurance and managed to help Mary over the initial shock and helped her to come to terms with her loneliness and unhappiness. At one stage, Mary thought that she would like to become a Catholic as she knew that it gave her some kind of peace and comfort. However, after several weeks, she realised that Duncan and Louise needed her as well and, with all the strength and effort that she could muster, she returned home with a determination to pick up the threads of her life.

A couple of weeks after Mary's return home, she decided that the time had come to have a talk with Duncan about their future.

'Duncan, I am sorry but I just cannot live in this house surrounded by all the memories of Julie. I cleared all her soft toys and most of her clothes away yesterday, but that still does not take away my memories and they fill this house.'

'I know, darling, how you feel. I feel bad enough myself, but that will be nothing compared to the pain that you are having to endure. I realise that you will not want to live here any longer and I intend to go to the estate agents tomorrow and put our house on the market.'

Duncan was filled with compassion for Mary and went over to her and held her close, without words. He felt for the first time that she was holding back from him – even rejecting him – but it was a feeling that he had never experienced before.

After this blow, another one was to follow quickly on its heels. Duncan was called to London to work at the Air Ministry as by now World War Two had broken out and England was at war with Germany. The Air Ministry wanted Duncan to requisition land for use by the American Air Force. This meant a whole new life was opening up for Duncan in London, with new friends and places, plus being in the midst of the action in wartime in the capital.

When Duncan and Mary had completed lengthy discussions, it was decided that Mary and Louise would stay in the North with Dr and Mrs Hunt, until they could be together again as a united little family.

The shock of Julie's death and its aftermath did not make it too difficult for Mary to agree to live for the time being at her parents' home and, in some ways, she welcomed it, as with her father being a doctor and police surgeon, it made Mary feel some kind of security, which was now sadly lacking in her life. This decision also made Duncan able to depart for London with a certain amount of peace of mind, knowing how well his wife and young daughter would be looked after and sheltered by the kindly Hunts.

As Duncan drove to London in his little Austin, he felt completely and utterly alone. His parting from Mary had proved to be a mixture of emotions. In fact, he did not realise until it actually happened, how easy the parting had seemed. Although he would not admit it, the parting had come somewhat as a relief because ever since Julie's death, he sensed that Mary was growing further away from him, both physically and emotionally. There were no tears from Mary and no whispered words of longing for his return.

In fact, if Duncan had to be completely honest to himself, Mary had seemed relieved at his parting, just as much as he had been. Since Julie's death, Duncan sensed that Mary was her own person, who needed her own space and her own time in which to develop a new personality. At first Duncan had found this new Mary hard to accept and he sometimes felt lonely and depressed, but in another way, he understood completely how Mary must feel. Mary had given birth to their child, had had her growing inside her for nine months and then she had had to experience the trauma of having it all taken away from her after a few short months of Julie's life. She could not, or would not, accept the damage that it had done to her.

Duncan's journey to London soon passed and he found quite easily the digs that the Air Ministry had booked for him. It was a large house in Collingham Gardens, which had been converted into bedsits. He parked his car opposite the house and arrived at the reception hall with his luggage.

'Hello,' he said to a tiny, neat, little lady, who would

prove to be his landlady and friend over the next couple of years. 'I am Duncan Robson and I hope you have a room ready for me.'

'Of course I have, Mr Robson. Your room is up on the second floor and I hope you will be comfortable here with us. We have a communal lounge and we pride ourselves on a little bar and a restaurant and so, if you are not eating out and would like a meal here, you just have to let us know in the morning.'

'Well, that sounds great,' replied Duncan. 'Sorry, but I do not know your name?'

'I am Mrs Harris, but seeing you will be living under my roof, you can call me Ruth, like the rest of my tenants do!'

Ruth then proceeded to take Duncan up two flights of stairs to his room.

'There is a bathroom and toilet on your landing and there is a public call box a hundred yards up the road. Turn left outside the house and it is situated on our side.

Duncan's room appeared clean but very basic, with the bed dominating the room, a far cry from home, but by the time he had put some books on display and some photographs of Mary and Louise, it would begin to look more like home.

Before leaving Duncan to unpack his things, Ruth said she would prepare him an evening meal and asked if there was any kind of food he did not like.

'No, I am very easy to please. It is all down to my Yorkshire upbringing! My mother always expected my two brothers and myself to eat anything and everything which was put down in front of us.' After a good meal and with all his unpacking completed, Duncan spent his first night in his new surroundings and slept exceptionally well.

Duncan took to his life in the Air Ministry like a duck

takes to water – in fact, within a few weeks, Duncan could hardly imagine that he had ever worked or, for that matter, ever lived, anywhere else than London. He felt utterly at home in his new environment. Sometimes he had to write himself a note to telephone Mary in Leeds to enquire how she and Louise were – they had both become more a part of his past and featured less and less in his life as he was living it now. At times this worried Duncan and he had to look at their photographs to get all their lives into perspective.

Chapter Five

Life spent in London became routine. Duncan would have his breakfast and then leave his digs at about a quarter past eight. He would catch a bus to the Aldwych and journey to his office at the Air Ministry. His work there proved to be interesting, he met a lot of people and got through an enormous amount of work. Duncan very easily made friends and he often went out to lunch or for a drink with his various colleagues.

One afternoon, when he was about to leave work for home, one of his friends, David Hall, came into his office and invited Duncan to go back for a bite of supper to his flat in Sloane Square. Duncan welcomed this kind invitation and accepted it without the slightest hesitation. He left the office with David and they made their way to the tube station to catch a train to Sloane Square.

David's flat was most impressive – it was very spacious, very light and bright, and to Duncan it appeared the real man about town's pad. As they entered the lounge, a cheerful female voice called out from the kitchen, 'I will only be a few minutes, Dave. I am just in the throes of turning the roast potatoes over!'

The smell of a roast cooking was very welcoming and Duncan thought the voice sounded rather nice too! David took Duncan on a conducted tour of his flat, having already poured him out a large gin and tonic. The flat was really very large and the kitchen was enormous, with a breakfast area included. If the voice which had called sounded good, well the owner of it was really lovely! A woman of about twenty-five years old, with dark wavy hair, a beautiful figure and brilliant blue eyes, was busy dealing with their evening meal.

David said, 'Duncan, I would like you to meet my sister, Anne.'

'Hello, Duncan. It's good to meet you.'

They shook hands warmly and Duncan was aware of a tremendous feeling of relief when he learned that Anne was indeed David's sister and not his girlfriend.

'I look after David and share his flat while we are both working here in London – I have a job with the BBC and living here suits me fine, and I guess David likes having someone looking after him whom he's used to.'

Duncan felt instantly drawn to Anne and felt sharp pangs of guilt knowing that, as a married man with a five year old daughter living in Leeds, he was not supposed to have this feeling of instant attraction.

'It's good to meet you, Anne, and equally good of David to invite me here to enjoy a meal with you both.'

Not only was Anne good to look at and to talk to, but she could cook well! The three of them spent a lovely evening. They chatted as if they were old friends and the evening passed by all too quickly. They had many interests in common, music being a favourite with the three of them and they ended the evening listening to records and promising themselves that they would go to the next concert at the Royal Albert Hall, when there was a programme on to suit them.

This was the evening that would change the whole of Duncan's life and, if he could have seen into the future, with all its hurts and frustrations, he would have settled for a quiet evening in his digs with his pipe, a good book and his radio for company.

His journey home was a mixture of happiness, excitement and, above all, anticipation. Try as he could, Duncan could not get Anne out of his mind – she was sexy, friendly and warm. When he arrived back at his digs, he got undressed and into bed, but sleep eluded him. He longed for the morning to arrive, so he could get to the office and see David to thank him for the previous evening. But most of all, Duncan wanted to set the wheels in motion for that promised trip, which they had talked about, to the Albert Hall. In fact, he decided to telephone the Albert Hall to ask for their list of forthcoming events – there was certainly no way that Duncan was going to let this opportunity slip away!

Ideas and thoughts were racing around and around in Duncan's head and he imagined he had Anne alone with him in the wilds of Scotland, staying in a remote hunting lodge or spending a few days in an old house on the cliffs somewhere in Cornwall. Duncan had a very romantic streak in him, but as yet, it had never surfaced, except in his fantasies.

His longing for and desire for Anne began on that very first meeting. These were different feelings from those he had had when he first met Mary, but Mary had definitely been right for him then. Duncan had changed, along with countless thousands of other people working and living away from home during this wretched war. Anne had awakened every possible desire in Duncan and he wanted to get to know her so much that it physically hurt him. He knew beyond a doubt that destiny had brought them together and that, however wrong it was, he wanted to get to know her in every sense of the word.

Chapter Six

The war continued; the bombing of London was grim and the sound of the sirens became as frequent as the ring of the telephone in peacetime. People in London were brave. They accepted death and yet they still fought on. Duncan hated the destruction that he saw all around him but he still accepted that his place of work was in the Air Ministry, right in the thick of the action. He now found he had no desire whatsoever to go back to Leeds and even the odd weekend visit became a strain.

By now, six months after his first meeting with Anne, they had become lovers. He adored her and she him in return. Neither of them dared to think of the war ending and, as a result, having to leave London. Anne had now rented a little flat in Redcliffe Gardens and had moved there so that she could be free to see Duncan whenever possible. David was against the whole idea and had told his sister over and over again that Duncan was a married man and that he would be going back to his wife and child when the war ended. But Anne could see no end to her love for Duncan and told David to leave her to sort things out herself. Despite this, David warned her at every opportunity that he could find. He even tried to reason with Duncan, but by now the pair were so besotted with each other that he might as well have saved his breath.

'I know this may sound possessive, Duncan, but I want

to be with you at every opportunity I possibly can and by having the flat, my own home, we are no longer flaunting our relationship.

Duncan looked at her and replied, 'I understand exactly how you feel, darling, really I do. I know that by taking the flat you have given us the chance we needed to be together without the interruptions from any outsiders. You must know how grateful I am to you for doing all this.'

'I just wish that you would move in with me, Duncan, instead of all this back and forth business,' Anne said pleadingly.

'You must understand that I would if I could, but it just isn't possible. If I did come to live here with you, I would have to explain to Mary why I left my digs, and I don't want to give her any cause for suspicion.'

Anne gazed back at her lover and answered, 'I could never begin to explain my feelings for you; you are my soul mate. All I can say is that when you're not here with me I feel so lonely. Even though outwardly I appear the same, I'm not the same person, and I doubt very much whether I ever will be again. The loneliness gives me an empty feeling inside which is only driven away when I am with you again.'

Somehow the war had lulled them into a false sense of security and neither of them could see an end to their present way of life at all. In fact, Duncan was convinced that no two people had ever loved each other as they did, and therefore that alone was a good enough reason for their love to continue for ever. The future, when it did loom up, just did not bear thinking about and they certainly had no intention of letting it spoil their time together.

Duncan's work was interesting and he requisitioned many houses, flats and suitable landing strips for the air force. He was mostly involved with the American Air Force, although he did the same work for the British. He even had the great honour of meeting the future president of the United States, Dwight Eisenhower, and was invited to dinner one evening at the American Embassy and later to a Sunday lunch at Eisenhower's lovely little hideaway, a cottage which was just off Kingston Hill. Duncan found his way there very easily as he had only recently got hold of some flats at Putney Heath and so he had already made several trips out in the Kingston direction on business.

Another great character whom Duncan met was the flying ace, Douglas Bader, and, although it was only a brief meeting, he was impressed by this incredibly brave man who had lost both his legs as a result of a daredevil prank at an airfield. The fact that he had had to have artificial legs had certainly done nothing to deter him, nor spoil his flying skills. He was an air ace in every sense of the word and such a likeable man as well.

Duncan was very thankful that he had been qualified as a chartered surveyor, as this profession held him in good stead for the work that was expected of him. Many men at the Ministry picked his brains and a lot of people were referred to him when others drew a blank.

The bombs continued to batter London. One day there was a bus, full of passengers, travelling along the Strand when a doodlebug gave it a direct hit and, although many people rushed to the scene, the bus, with all its passengers, was never seen again. In fact, it was so incredible that not even a button was ever found; the bus including the crew and passengers just vanished off the face of the earth. Duncan and Anne had been walking in the direction of the Strand when the tragedy occurred and had joined the other rescuers, but there was absolutely nothing there and they were both badly shaken up by the incident.

Anne said on the way back to her flat, 'Duncan, when something happens like this, it makes me realise that we are all so vulnerable and it makes me want to hold on to you more and more.'

'Darling, we have to make the most of every day and night of our lives,' replied Duncan. 'None of us know how long we have got and the war exaggerates it. All I do know is that we have all got jobs to do and I love you with all my heart. That gives me two good reasons to want to survive all this destruction which is going on around us.'

The weeks dragged on and their lives took on a pattern – Duncan worked all day at the Air Ministry or was out and about visiting possible sites, whilst Anne continued with her job at the BBC as an assistant in the news department. Both were very absorbed in their jobs when they were there, but their greatest times were when they were together in the evenings or at weekends. Their times together were fairly restricted, though, as Anne was often working late at the BBC and Duncan often had to stay on late at his office. Weekends did not always prove to be convenient either, as Duncan occasionally had to go home to Leeds and stay the odd night with his family; however, these trips up North became fewer and fewer and he found he was already having to make excuses why he could not get home for a particular weekend.

The bombing in Leeds was getting fairly heavy, so Dr Hunt had arranged for Mary and Louise, together with his younger daughter and her two children, to go and live for a while at a farm that he owned up on the moors at Pately Bridge. Dr Hunt felt they would be a great deal safer there rather than living in Leeds. Mary, although she did not care for the idea, packed her things and settled for the last part of the war to be with her sister and her family at Pately Bridge.

It actually proved to be a good move. The sisters enjoyed being together and the children had fun being on the farm and living in the country for a while. It was a particularly good time for Louise as her cousins, who were very close to her age, were constant playmates and it was the closest that she got to having a brother and sister. They drank fresh milk, and even learnt to milk the cows, which was quite a challenge for them with their small hands! They ate homemade butter, which the farmer's wife made with great expertise.

They also had lovely eggs, which they collected daily from the hens and which were often still warm. It was a very happy part of Louise's young life and one which she often referred to in her adult years. Dr Hunt used to drive out whenever possible to visit them and go back to Leeds laden with the fresh produce from his farm. The children thrived during their time on the farm and even had a little Wendy house to play in. The farm had no bathroom and so, when they needed a bath, a tin bathtub was dragged down in front of the open fire and filled with endless kettles of boiling water, the children being bathed in turn. It certainly was a far cry from their lives in Leeds!

Chapter Seven

The year of 1945 arrived and, with it, the general feeling that the war was drawing to its conclusion. The time was also fast approaching when Duncan and Anne had to face the future and decide what was going to happen to them.

One evening Duncan arrived at Anne's flat and, after a rather subdued dinner, they sat down either side of the fireplace and attempted to sort out their future.

'I hardly dare ask you what is going to happen to us when the war is over,' Anne used as an opening remark.

Duncan thought for a while. 'It's strange, but although I want to see an end to the war, in many ways I dread it. I have hidden behind the war years for so long and probably I have been happier than ever before in my life because of you, my darling Anne.'

Duncan walked over to the sideboard and poured them both a glass of port.

'I know we have discussed this all before, but my duty is to remain married to Mary. It was not her fault that I met you and I have absolutely no right to let her down. You are the best thing that ever happened to me, Anne, but I'm not free to spend the rest of my life with you. My guilt is always with me these days, but even that doesn't outweigh my love for you.'

Duncan had already decided that there was no way that he wanted to return to live in the North. He had by now grown very attached to London and the South and he had no desire whatsoever to go back to the industrial gloom of the North. He had previously made up his mind that he would purchase a home plus a surveying business in London, the nearer the heart of London the better. This in itself was not surprising as he had lived and worked in London now for the past six years.

Anne was both surprised and disappointed that at this stage Duncan had no intention at all of asking Mary for a divorce, so that he would be left free to marry her. At first, this fact would just not sink in and she felt that, after all they had been to each other, Duncan owed it to her to be with her.

Duncan explained as carefully as he could that he wanted their love affair to continue, but that he did not see why, in the process, he needed to hurt Mary and his daughter by leaving them both. After all, they were the innocent parties in all of this, and had it not been for the war, he and Anne would never have met each other.

'But the war did happen and we did meet and we did fall in love,' protested Anne, who was by now getting a feeling of uncontrollable panic that Duncan was actually going to end it all with her.

Their first real argument now took place. The secure feelings which they had had for each other up until now were quite definitely being threatened and neither of them could change some of the things they were saying to each other.

Duncan said, 'Anne, you have just got to accept the facts and see it from my point of view. After all, we both knew that I was married when we first met and you were quite prepared to agree then.'

'Yes, I was prepared to accept it then', replied Anne, 'but

surely, after all we've been through and all the love we've given to each other, surely you can't toss me aside like an old glove?'

'I have no intention of doing that. I just want us to go on loving each other but without having to hurt Mary and Louise. They don't know about us, so why shatter their lives by telling them now?'

At this stage, something bordering on suspicion hit Anne and she took a long hard look at Duncan before saying, 'Duncan, for the last few years I have given you my heart and even possibly my soul. Do you honestly intend for us to keep seeing one another on the same basis for the rest of our lives? Do you really think that you can live your life pleasing your wife and daughter and having me hidden away in order to snatch a few hours of love when it suits you, that is, providing that you will have the time left to fit me into your future plans?'

The conversation between the two lovers continued in this vein for another hour or two. But try as she might, Anne couldn't alter Duncan's view of their future life together and he showed no intention of backing down. Anne realised that, however much she loved him, Duncan was basically a coward and couldn't face the upset of breaking completely with his past life and hurting all the people who went to make up his pre-war existence. But Anne had got to the point where she wanted Duncan entirely to herself. She was also in a much better position as she was single and had very few family ties. She had her brother, David, and a widowed mother who lived in Brighton and whom she saw very rarely.

Anne hadn't been unattractive to other suitors, but Duncan had that certain something which had captivated her completely. Maybe in the beginning she was drawn by the fact that he was unattainable because he was already married, but as the months passed, he became her very reason for living and she now had no intention of letting him go.

This evening proved fraught with tension and, when the time came for him to return to his digs, they were drained of all emotion except to bid one another a sad 'good night'. Neither of them had any fight left in them and they had exchanged enough words to give them plenty of food for thought.

Chapter Eight

The following morning in the aftermath of Duncan and Anne's discussion, Duncan did some very serious thinking regarding his future. He put a call through to Mary who was by now back in Leeds and installed with her parents once more. He just briefly told her that he needed to talk to her regarding their future plans and that he had booked a seat on the train North on Friday night, so that they could discuss everything thoroughly. Mary seemed quite pleased that he was coming up North to sort out their lives and said that she would be at Leeds station to meet him. He then phoned Anne. 'Hello Anne, I'm just calling you to let you know that I'm going up to Leeds on Friday and will be spending the weekend with the family. I want a chance to talk to Mary and plan the next move. I love you and you must hold on to that and trust me. I will phone you Sunday evening on my return to London.'

Anne found nothing to say except, 'All right, Duncan, do what you have to do but remember that I love you. You are my whole life.'

With those few words, she put the telephone receiver down.

When Duncan got to the train on Friday, he felt a sense of release. He couldn't describe the feeling but it was as though some bolt that had been tightly closed had just suddenly been released. He now had a little breathing space, time to think on his own without being interrupted. He hadn't seen Mary for about five months and wondered what kind of reception he would receive from her as they had grown so far apart. Their lives had hardly crossed during the last six years and the gap was getting wider. He thought of Louise, his only child; he realised in horror that he hardly knew her and that he must appear almost a stranger to her. Her grandfather, Dr Hunt, would have been her proxy father and Duncan was just a man whose voice she heard occasionally on the other end of the telephone. He wondered how Mary had coped with this situation. He knew his daughter would be loved and well cared for as the Hunts were a very close family. The bond between a child and its parents is formed at such an early age and he and Louise had certainly missed out on that score.

The train journey passed uneventfully and, after he had eaten a reasonable dinner in the dining car, the train was approaching Leeds. Duncan took his case down from the rack, put his coat on and prepared to disembark. Leeds station was cold after the warmth of the train, but there, waiting at the barrier, was Mary and she was waving to him. After giving him a brief kiss on his cheek, she led him out of the station and into the waiting car. As her father was the City Police Surgeon he had sent Mary with one of his drivers to meet Duncan.

The family were all pleased to see Duncan and they all had a nightcap and made light conversation as it was now getting on for midnight and they were all tired. Duncan followed Mary up to her bedroom and was surprised and somewhat hurt to realise that she made no attempt whatsoever to embrace him or show any signs of endearment. By now he had grown accustomed to Anne throwing her arms around him as soon as she saw him. However, Mary made no such gestures and, quite the contrary, indicated that he should keep his distance. He unpacked quickly and got into his own bed. Meanwhile Mary was giving the impression of being sound asleep by the time he returned from the bathroom. Their years apart had really taken their toll on the relationship.

The morning arrived and when Duncan opened his eyes there was a little girl watching him intently.

'Hello, Louise, and how's the world treating you?' enquired Duncan.

She just grinned and said, 'Hello; I'm fine. Granny wants to know if you would like a cooked breakfast or just toast?'

'Just toast and coffee, please, and I'll be down in about half an hour.'

Louise nodded her head and skipped out of the room. How strange, thought Duncan, that little girl is my own daughter and she talked to me just as though I was an ordinary house guest!

After breakfast, Mary told Duncan that she had arranged for them to go and see his parents as they were anxious to see him once more and that they had been invited there for lunch. The day passed pleasantly enough and yet all the time Duncan was aware that Mary was holding him at arm's length. Duncan's reason for his trip home was to talk out his future plans with his wife and she was giving him very little time to do so. Nevertheless, the opportunity did arise and that evening, after dinner, the Hunts retired to the study to give Mary and Duncan plenty of time to talk.

'Well, Mary, it looks as if, after all these years apart, we are a lot nearer to becoming that united little family again.'

'Yes. It looks that way, Duncan,' replied Mary.

'I want to tell you, Mary, that I have no desire to come back to live and work in Leeds. I would like to stay in London and establish my own surveying business there. I have many contacts and I know that being in London will make me far more successful than being in business here. I also have the chance to rent a luxury flat in Putney Heath – one in a block that I requisitioned for the Americans and they have promised me one if I want to have it.'

'If it is what you really want to do, Duncan, then I am prepared to go along with all your suggestions. After all, when I left school, I was sent to a finishing school in Wimbledon and I had a wonderful year there. Putney Heath is no stranger to me as it is all in that Wimbledon area, which I grew so used to.'

They talked on and on well into the early hours of the following morning and it was decided that Duncan should go ahead with all his working and living plans and then send for Mary and Louise when he was ready for them to join him, after he had sorted out their home and found suitable offices.

Duncan returned to London the following afternoon with peace of mind regarding Mary's attitude to their future, but wondering how on earth he was ever going to sort out his other life, the one he had with Anne.

Chapter Nine

By the time Duncan arrived on Anne's doorstep, she had well and truly decided what line of action she was going to take! She welcomed Duncan as usual with open arms and also felt relieved to see him again. He could not help but compare the different greetings that he had received from Anne and Mary, one so warm and loving and the other cold and remote, but with respect. Duncan could not blame Mary for her offhand attitude to him. After all, he had made very little attempt to see her over the past six years, she was still an attractive young woman and she probably felt that he was rejecting her. He had invented quite a few reasons why he could not get home more often.

Anne, in contrast, was overjoyed to see him and he felt he had been away for a month rather than for a couple of nights!

'Duncan, you have no idea how long these last two nights have seemed to me. You will never know just how much I miss you when you are away from me.'

'I have missed you too and it is a wonderful feeling to have you back in my arms again.'

Anne had a gorgeous meal awaiting him and she had made herself look more attractive than usual. His heart certainly warmed to her and yet he felt guilty that he was unable now to feel this warmth for Mary.

After their meal Duncan kept his promise and told Anne what he had discussed with Mary and how she had agreed to come to London when he had got everything sorted out for her here. Duncan held his breath and waited for Anne to tell him to leave, but quite the reverse; she got on the floor and put her head on his knees and hugged him.

'I could never leave you, Duncan, and if you still want me, I will always be here for you. I can never imagine my life without you and I could never settle for anyone else. After all that I said to you, I do understand that you owe your first loyalty to your wife and daughter, but I can't bear to let you go. The only way I could ever let go would be if you told me to.'

Duncan put his arms around her and said, 'I could never tell you to go, Anne. I love you more than I thought it was ever possible to love another human being, but I also know that I am being unfair to you and also to Mary. I realise that I will have to live with this feeling over the years and I just hope that it will all work out for us. I promise you here and now that I will never ask you to leave me and that I will always come to you whenever you need me.'

Anne told Duncan of the agonising weekend she had just spent wondering what he was saying to his family and whether they would persuade him to go back to live in Leeds and to work there.

'I didn't know if this dinner tonight was going to be the start of our next few years together or if it was going to be the end of what we have already shared.'

By now, great big tears were rolling uncontrollably down Anne's cheeks and Duncan, sensing her vulnerability, came down beside her and took her fully in his arms and made love to her as he had never done before. He felt how small and insecure she was, knowing then how he had to be strong enough to cope with this situation.

Their relationship up until now had always been full of fun and happiness and Duncan decided that he would really have to work hard to keep it happy and free from as much frustration as possible. He also knew that the coming years would never be as happy as these war years had proved to be for them. His wife and child had seemed so far away, but soon they would be here and needing his time and attention.

The war officially ended in September 1945, and Duncan and Anne joined the crowds who thronged outside Buckingham Palace. It really was a celebration en masse and the crowds went wild with excitement as the king and queen appeared with the two princesses on the balcony, time and time again, each time the cheers seeming louder than the ones before!

The excitement for Duncan and Anne, however, was overshadowed by a wave of sadness. This was the end of their time of being free to see each other whenever possible. They both sensed that it was the end of a chapter and the start of the unknown where lies and deceit would have to take a dominant part in their future lives. Anne would have loved him to run away with her there and then but she knew beyond any doubt that, although she was convinced of Duncan's love for her, she also knew that he hadn't the strength to break away from his family ties.

But it was no use being troubled tonight. It was a time for celebration and thankfulness that they had come through the war in bomb-ridden London without being hurt. Tonight was special and the atmosphere around them was electric. The crowds linked arms and sang, danced and generally went wild in celebration of their country's victory.

Duncan and Anne returned to Anne's flat happy, tired and full of apprehension for the years that lay ahead of them.

Chapter Ten

The next few months filled Duncan's mind with plans. He would wake up in the night, think of another idea, reach for a notebook and pencil and jot the idea down there and then, just in case he had forgotten it by the time the morning arrived.

His first aim was to secure the flat in Putney which he had set his heart on having for his wife and daughter. This, as it so happened, proved to be a very straightforward transaction and the flat became his by the end of November. It was a large three-bedroom flat on the ground floor and it overlooked a large square lawn which had flower beds and shrubs and was very attractively laid out. The flats, about ninety of them, overlooked the garden on three sides as the flats were divided into three blocks. Behind the flats, which looked up towards the road, was a huge communal garden with two tennis courts and so the tenants had plenty of garden for sitting and walking in and, with the Heath just over the other side of the road, it all went to make a pleasant setting. These flats had appealed to Duncan from the very first time he had seen them.

Duncan telephoned Mary to tell her of his good fortune in securing the flat. 'Mary, I am phoning you to let you know that the flat in Putney Heath is now ours! If you would like to come to London, I will then take you and show you our new home and then you can make all the necessary arrangements.'

Mary replied, 'Thank you for letting me know and I will telephone you soon to let you know what day and also what train I will be coming on.'

They also agreed not to move in until the New Year as the upheaval would prove too great just before Christmas.

The acquisition of the flat at Putney Heath was Duncan's first part of his plan successfully completed and now he had to get himself established in a firm of surveyors in London. As it turned out, this also fell into place quickly because, having been in London, living and working for the past six years, Duncan knew the right people to get in contact with. He joined a firm near to Marble Arch. It was not a large firm but Duncan saw many possibilities for future expansion and, above all, he was in the heart of town where he had always aimed to be.

Duncan felt a relief and also a sense of satisfaction that the family and business sides of his life had all slotted neatly into place. He now had to start sorting out his future lifestyle with Anne, which would prove somewhat more difficult. She was living in the same little flat as she had been throughout the war years, but she had now become restless and wanted a change of scenery. She and Duncan had lengthy talks concerning the best place for her to move to. They decided that it would have to be somewhere within easy access of London as Anne was still working at the BBC in Langham Place, which was near Oxford Circus. Also her future home had to be convenient not only for work, but also for Duncan to continue to visit her without too much time being wasted on travelling to and from his firm.

After several weeks of looking around in different districts, Anne found a little semidetached house in North

Harrow quite near to the station and well away from Putney; about fifteen miles separated the areas. Anne felt that, having spent the war years in London, she now wanted room to breathe a little fresh air and she liked the idea of a little house with a garden of her own. She also needed a home where Duncan would be welcomed and loved away from his family and business ties. Duncan was always foremost in her mind and she still lived in the hope that he would one day come to her completely. She loved him with all her heart and soul and would accept him on any terms as life without him would mean nothing to her. The two lovers continued to meet after work and had many discussions on their future lives.

'Anne, you really have made a good choice regarding the house. It is perfect for what you need and I know that I am going to look forward to being part of your life there. I love you for making all this possible. I only wish I could be with you all the time. If only I had met you before I met Mary.'

'Duncan, please don't say things like that, because you did meet Mary first and I certainly would not want you to become bitter about her. We will just have to make the best of what time we have together.'

Mary arrived in London in the January of 1946, and she arrived alone as they agreed that it was best for Louise to stay with her grandparents until the flat was ready and all their belongings well and truly sorted out.

The biggest indication that all was not well was when Mary insisted that she and Duncan had separate bedrooms. She made the lame excuse that she had got used to sleeping on her own during the past six years and she knew how late into the night Duncan read his books and consequently kept his bedside light on. This suggestion took Duncan by surprise, but he thought it best to agree with her, rather than create a scene; he also thought that maybe in time she'd want him back with her again, although he had his doubts. He had rather expected her to request separate beds, but nevertheless was surprised when the request was made for separate rooms! So, when they moved into their flat, it was also into their own bedrooms. Certainly, in Anne's home, they shared not only the same bedroom but a large, comfortable double bed.

Anne had settled into the house in North Harrow extremely well, but always with the longing to have Duncan with her. However, a few hours of his company were better than the alternative, which she did not care to contemplate. Duncan had bought Anne and himself this house but had had it put in his name and had promised her that he would leave strict instructions in his will that the house and all its contents would come to her if he died before her. So he told her that she was not to worry as she would never be without a home. This gave Anne a funny feeling as it felt as if she were married to Duncan but of course she knew she was not. She also realised that Duncan was trying to make her feel very loved and secure and, for his thoughtfulness to her, she loved him even more, if it was at all possible. She had not done anything in this house without his full approval, even asking him to take the final decision on the colour of the saucepans! Anne so desperately needed to feel that it was their home and not just hers.

Meanwhile, Mary had got their flat in Putney looking very nice and their furniture, which had been in store during the war years, was brought down from Leeds. The Hunts brought Louise down at the end of March and she went wild with excitement at seeing her mother, though she was more noticeably reserved when greeting her father but that was only to be expected after a six-year gap of continuous communication in their lives.

Duncan's life slowly but surely fell into a routine. The routine was laced with a good deal of deceit but nevertheless a routine was firmly established. Mary, for some reason, accepted this pattern of his life without question, very much to the surprise and relief of Duncan, who had anticipated a great deal of opposition on Mary's part.

On Monday mornings, Duncan would go off to his office from Putney and on Thursdays he would return home in time for dinner. He always made a point of phoning Mary each day, sometimes twice, but never in the evenings and also he never left a number where he could be contacted – it was always Duncan who made the calls. If, on very rare occasions, Mary needed to phone, she left a message at his office, but if any emergency had ever occurred at night, it would have been impossible to contact him as Mary had no idea at all where he was. Luckily there was never any cause to phone him after office hours. Duncan's explanation for his absence at the beginning of each week was that his business took him to all parts of the country and he would stay in hotels in the town or city where he had had his last appointment. But the truth was that he would make quite sure that he completed his appointments in good time to get back to Anne in North Harrow for his evening meal and then spend the night in her arms in their bed. Anne, in turn, had no choice but to settle for this arrangement. She still would dearly have loved him to marry her, but was resigned to the thought that he would not. Mentally, Duncan continued to stimulate her and physically he satisfied her and so the subject of marriage between them was now a closed book and the strain, in turn, had lifted from their relationship.

How often they longed to be back in the war days when they spent every night together.

Guilt now was always with Duncan but even that feeling he had had to come to terms with, as it was a negative emotion and he was a positive-thinking man. But he built up a wall around him so that even his own daughter could not get close to him. He always had a fear of Louise finding out about his guilty secret – he had to admit to himself that he dreaded her finding out even more than he did Mary.

Chapter Eleven

It started out to be such a very ordinary Monday morning. Duncan cheerfully kissed Mary and Louise goodbye and steered his car into the traffic towards Marble Arch. He was not feeling smug at the thought of escaping after the weekend to see Anne, although he had certainly missed her since last Thursday. It was more a feeling of freedom which he always experienced when driving his car; it was good to be on his own for a while with just his thoughts, and he had the radio on quietly in the background.

Duncan was mentally working out what he had planned for the day ahead. Firstly a visit to his office to sort out the post and then he would dictate any necessary replies. He had arranged a lunchtime meeting at the Cumberland Hotel with a solicitor from Bond Street – a nice man, but rather dull and pompous, but no doubt a good lunch with some wine would ease the way! Duncan smiled to himself. Considering life was complicated, it was also very good and he still enjoyed all that he packed into it very much. He had to visit a site in Reading in the afternoon, but he would still be finished in time to return to Anne's for dinner. Poor Anne, he thought, weekends must drag for her with him away, but he would soon remedy that this evening.

Suddenly, with no warning whatsoever, a huge lorry completely out of control came careering down on the other side of the road. Duncan had no time to swing out of its path as it veered across the central reservation and ran smashing into Duncan's Rover head on. Duncan's last thought was of complete helplessness and then it all went black and was all over for him.

Mary received the news from a very kindly policewoman who arrived on the doorstep at about half past ten. The policewoman asked Mary if she could come inside and talk to her.

'Of course,' said Mary, and she led her into the lounge.

'Please will you sit down,' requested the policewoman of Mary. 'I am afraid I have some very distressing news for you.' Mary did not have any time in which to think what it could be that she was about to learn.

'I am very sorry to tell you, Mrs Robson, and there is no easy way to do it, but your husband was killed in a car accident on his way to work this morning. He would have died instantly as it was a lorry that lost control and drove head on into your husband's car. I can however assure you that it would have all been over so fast that he would not have felt anything or had time to understand what was happening.'

Mary's shock was immense and she could hardly comprehend what she had heard. Duncan was so alive and so very healthy just over an hour ago and now it seemed impossible that in that short time his life could have been so cruelly ended.

After the policewoman had gone, Mary telephoned Duncan's parents and told them the awful news and then told her own parents. Mary did not relish the thought of telling Louise when she returned home from school. It seemed ironical that Duncan had spent the war years here in the Home Guard in London, avoiding bombs, being in the very thick of danger and managing to survive it all, only to be killed in a road accident two years later on. Mary could make no sense of it. She felt completely numb from shock, but, when she had telephoned her parents in Leeds to tell them of the tragedy, they immediately said they would be coming down to London on the first available train and would prove, as always in her life, to be Mary's towers of strength.

Telling Louise was quite a different matter. Louise was now a happy and confident twelve year old; she enjoyed her school work and, although she was an average pupil, she proved very popular with both her peers and the staff and had adjusted to her life in London very well. Her father's death came as a bitter blow to her as she felt that she was just beginning to get to know him. Grandpa Hunt had always been the man in her life, but since leaving Yorkshire she had liked her new environment and enjoyed being with her father, even though Duncan had kept her somewhat at arm's length. Sometimes at weekends he would take her on to the heath and, armed with the *Observer Book of Trees*, he explained and taught Louise which trees were which. She loved these expeditions together and went home and wrote all about what she had learnt from Duncan. He also took her to places like Hampton Court Palace or Kew Gardens on a Sunday morning whilst Mary cooked their roast dinner. There was a definite bond starting to grow between father and daughter and now it had been bitterly severed forever.

Mary also felt the blow; she never professed to being close to Duncan these days but she was used to him and content and relaxed in his company. In some respects, now it was as if it had all been pointless for her coming to live in London. She had grown so used to being up in Yorkshire with her young daughter and elderly parents, that the upheaval now seemed as though it should never have been allowed to happen. It would have been easier for her if she had remained in Yorkshire with Louise and for Duncan to have travelled home for the weekends. After all, his routine was to be away so much of the time in any case.

Although Mary took his death very badly, she still had a strange feeling that she had lost part of him in the war years and this had unknowingly prepared her for his actual death.

Dr and Mrs Hunt were so concerned how their daughter and young granddaughter would cope with Duncan's passing that they tried to make them talk about it to them as much as possible.

Mary said one evening, 'Please don't worry too much about us. I have always had a feeling that I lost Duncan a long time ago. Call it woman's intuition, but something or someone had taken him away from us during the war. Life was never the same with Duncan as it had been in the old days before the war and in some ways it has made me accept things a lot better.'

Mary was also happy not to probe and she certainly had no desire to delve into the unknown now he was gone. She literally accepted the situation as it was.

Chapter Twelve

Meanwhile, on the fateful day of Duncan's death, Anne had taken so much trouble to make sure that everything was just right for their evening together. There was a warm glow to her cheeks and she looked very attractive in her soft, clinging, black wool dress. She hummed a little tune to herself as she laid the table and stood back to admire her handiwork. She wanted everything to be just perfect this evening. She opened Duncan's favourite Beaujolais wine and left it to 'breathe' on the sideboard. She decided not to light the candles until Duncan arrived and they were having their pre-dinner drinks and all was under control. They would start with smoked salmon and prawns with the chilled German Niersteiner wine and then the Beaujolais would accompany the fillet steak, mushrooms and baked potatoes and then the meal would be rounded off with a selection of cheeses and coffee. This was always their favourite meal whenever they had something to celebrate.

Anne could hardly wait to hear Duncan's car draw up to the house! Not since she had heard the news on Friday from the hospital that she was pregnant and that the baby – their baby – was due in seven months time! Anne had no fear of telling Duncan she was carrying his baby. They had agreed during the last year that, if it happened, it happened. Anne was prepared to have a child and bring it up as a single mother. She wanted a part of Duncan to be with her at all times, a constant reminder of their deep love for one another.

She had certainly been feeling strange the last few weeks and now her feelings were a reality and the thought of their baby thrilled her. They would cope with any problems as they arose but now she was content and bubbling over with happiness. Usually Duncan arrived between seven o'clock and half past but, strangely, it was already half past seven. and there was no sign of him. When it got to eight o'clock Anne became increasingly worried. Duncan was always so punctual and, even if he knew that he was going to be even as little as ten minutes late, he would always phone to warn Anne. Maybe he has got into a traffic jam, thought Anne, and he has not been able to get to a phone box to let me know. She sat down and poured herself out a very weak Scotch with water. There was nothing else she could do but sit and wait and hope that he would not be much longer in arriving. Time ticked on slowly and it was not long before the waiting became unbearable. A sinking feeling came into the pit of her stomach. She even turned the record player off as the music began to irritate her and disturb her thoughts; her appetite and her enthusiasm of an hour ago had now all faded away.

As the time began to pass, the anxiety and fear deepened for Anne. It was now ten o'clock and there was still no sight nor sound of Duncan. The feeling of helplessness increased and, through desperation, Anne decided to phone Duncan's secretary, although she knew she would not in the ordinary way involve anyone else. She dialled the secretary's number and waited in fear and trembling for her to answer. At last, after several rings, a crisp, efficient voice answered with a Paddington number.

Anne quickly explained that she was a friend of

Duncan's and was expecting him to attend a dinner party and could not understand why he had failed to arrive. Anne tried to keep her voice cool and controlled, which she found extremely hard. She actually felt like choking over her words. She asked his secretary to check with his home to make sure all was well, and then asked her if she would be kind enough to telephone her back. When the secretary suggested that Anne should phone Duncan's home herself, she made an excuse that she had not got his number and that she must return to her other dinner guests. She just let her know her name was Anne.

After the call, the minutes dragged. Anne just could not understand how it could take Duncan's secretary so long to phone her back. The phone, in fact, did not ring until way after eleven o'clock and then the terrible truth was made known to Anne. Duncan's secretary said:

'Anne, I am afraid that I have just received the most appalling news from Mrs Robson. Duncan was in a car crash this morning as he was driving up to the office. Evidently a lorry lost control, coming into Duncan's car head on. He never stood a chance and the police said that he was killed outright. I can hardly believe it myself. I thought Duncan had gone on to a site somewhere this morning. I was not in the office this afternoon as I had a dental appointment and Duncan had given me the afternoon off. I feel shocked as he was a wonderful man to work for – I cannot take it all in. I am sorry to spoil your evening with this news.'

With this, Duncan's secretary was clearly crying when she hurriedly rang off. At first, Anne thought it was all some kind of bad dream and then the awful truth sank deeper in. Her pain, both physical and mental, was almost unbearable and reality failed to exist. Duncan had promised her time and time again that he would never ever leave her and now, through no fault of his own, he had done that very thing she feared.

Tonight of all nights she had imagined would have been the happiest of their lives and now it proved to be the end rather than a new beginning. Duncan would never know of his unborn child and it would be Anne's job and sole responsibility for the rest of her life, which now she was destined to cope with alone.

Chapter Thirteen

As Duncan had died in a car accident and had received many injuries, it was decided between the family that Mary should not go and see him prior to his funeral. Dr Hunt really insisted that, as always in the past, Mary should be protected – he had always had this strong protective feeling for his elder child, which, although he would never admit it to anyone, he did not have the same feeling for his other daughter. Mary was special to him, his first-born and he was immensely proud of her good looks and poise. He had always loved her dearly right from the moment she was born. He had continued to feel this way long after Mary had married Duncan, thus becoming a wife and mother herself.

Dr Hunt and his wife stayed with Mary and Louise and did everything in their power to comfort and console them. They were very saddened themselves as they had loved and admired Duncan who had been an exceptional man. He had had so many interests in life and could really talk on any subject which you had cared to choose. His knowledge of wines was astounding and he had taught many of his friends how to recognise the different ones and could tell them of their origin and the different areas where they were produced. His knowledge, he always confessed, came from his love of books. He read probably every day of his life. Books were his great love and never a day went by without him learning something new. His death seemed such a terrible waste as there was so much that he still would obviously have liked to have done.

A calmness and acceptance came over Mary. She felt she had to be strong for Louise because it had been such a shock to her as she was just getting used to the fact of having a father around. She had liked this feeling, so Mary comforted and consoled her young daughter, putting Louise's feelings before her own.

The day of the funeral dawned. It was a dismal day and never seemed to get light. The funeral was to be conducted shortly after lunch and then a few close friends and family would come back to the flat for a drink and sandwiches.

When Mary arrived in the chapel and took her place in the front pew with Louise and her parents, she felt very strange. She had walked through the chapel, which was packed with familiar faces, including business associates whom Mary had met from time to time. But what really had caused this strange feeling was a woman who was sitting all alone on a pew right at the back of the chapel. Mary did not know who this lady was but she felt that somehow she should have known her. She was sitting staring ahead with a desolate look, completely lost in her own private world. Mary almost stopped in her tracks to go over to her, but something made her continue to keep walking ahead.

The service itself was very moving. It was a real tribute to Duncan's life and his achievements, which was given by his elder brother, Graham. He gave thanks for Duncan's life and said how he had meant so much to all who had had the honour to know him. He had touched so many people's lives in his years on this earth.

After the service, the mourners moved outside and made

their way to the graveside where Duncan's coffin was lowered slowly into the ground. This was by far the most harrowing part of the whole funeral and Louise was almost uncontrollable in her grief. The tears poured down and the sobs shook the whole of her body. It was so very final, witnessing her father being lowered into the ground, the memory of which would remain with Louise for the rest of her life. Then they all went back to look at the many flowers and wreaths which had now been placed on the ground outside the chapel. There were so many moving messages written to Duncan and it produced some kind of relief to ease the pain and tension by reading the tributes and being able to admire the beautiful arrangements of flowers which had been sent from far and wide by so many caring people.

As Mary and Louise were standing by the flowers and talking to their numerous friends and family, they both became aware once more of the lone lady, who came up to the flowers, and they watched her place a single red rose amongst them and then she turned abruptly and walked away. The last sight Mary and Louise had of her, was of her walking down the avenue which led away from the chapel. She was completely alone, but Mary had a strong feeling that she had been very much a part of Duncan's life – the side of his life which Mary knew nothing at all about – and she suddenly felt a great sadness for this lonely woman. Mary was surrounded by so many people who consoled and loved her and Louise, which all helped to ease the pain, but this forlorn figure was noticeably alone and Mary had a very caring heart.

Part Two
Louise's Story

Chapter One

Having just spent a wakeful night tossing and turning, Louise was more than thankful when the morning eventually dawned. The entire night had seemed endless and sleep had eluded her. Mentally she had been so wide awake, yet physically her body had needed the refreshment that only sleep can produce.

The reason that Louise had spent such a bad night was the fact that she had had an emotional shock during the course of the previous evening. It had started simply enough with her mother, Mary, asking her to get a document from her writing desk and Louise, in the process of looking for it, had come across the handwritten copy of the will of her father, who had tragically died in a car crash six years earlier.

Louise was now nineteen years old. She had grown up into a lovely girl, brimming with health and vitality and she was very popular with her many friends. She lived at home with her mother and was a student at a college in South Kensington where she was studying journalism and secretarial skills. She was doing well and was enjoying her course a lot. The two-year course would stand her in good stead when the time came to start looking and applying for jobs. Her recreation hours were mostly spent playing tennis. She was an enthusiastic member of a local club where she had made many friends and enjoyed a full and happy social life. It was good to spend the afternoons at weekends playing tennis and then Saturday nights proved very sociable with the various wine and cheese parties and dances that the club arranged. There was always plenty to join in with. An extra bonus was that Louise was very friendly with a family whose house backed on to the club and so she would, more often than not, stay there on the Saturday night after the party. She was always welcomed as a second daughter into their household.

In the peace and quiet of last night, Louise had lain in bed thinking about her discovery. Her father's will had left her in no doubt whatsoever that her father had been very involved with another woman, called Anne Robson – her name had certainly dominated his will from start to finish. The very fact that the will had been handwritten indicated that it had been done this way so that their family solicitors would remain unaware of Anne's existence and of her father's involvement with her. Duncan would have hated that and he had obviously guarded his secret very well. He had been leading a double life, but equally he had made sure that his two lives would never clash. His handwritten will proved to be a natural result of this relationship with this other woman.

If her father's will had had this effect on Louise after all these years, she could very well imagine what a profound shock it must have been to her mother and to her grandparents, six years ago, when they had first read the will after Duncan's fatal car accident. What an added shock it must all have proved to be to them on top of Duncan's premature death. Her mother had always been such a lady, not only attractive to look at, but she was very gentle when dealing with people. She would have been horrified to discover that her husband had been deceiving her. An added insult had been that Anne's name had been mentioned foremost in Duncan's will and that Anne was firmly established as a Robson.

'I, Duncan James Robson, bequeath to Anne Elizabeth Robson, nee Hall, my house in Harrow, including all the contents therein, together with the sum of ten thousand pounds.'

The remainder of the will had benefited Mary and Louise, although Louise's share was to be tied up in a trust fund, so that the capital would be invested in order to provide Mary with an income for the rest of her life. Duncan had also stipulated that, in the unfortunate event of himself and Mary both being in a fatal accident, his estate would then have to be divided equally between Louise and Anne!

Louise's thoughts had rolled round and round; she felt as if she had been reading a story rather than reading her father's will. The more she thought about it, the more incredible it all seemed. Why had her father needed this Anne Robson in his life? Why, if he was so close to her, had he not left Mary and gone to live with her? Questions went whirling around in Louise's mind and the only person who could provide her with all the answers she needed had now been dead for the past six years.

To say that Louise was feeling puzzled was an understatement. Duncan's will had proved to be a painful discovery, and she wondered what havoc it had created in her mother's life. Mary had continued to be the perfect mother and friend to her as she had been before her father's death, but apparently she must have lived with the knowledge of Anne Robson's importance in her husband's life since the reading of the will. What a nightmare this knowledge would have produced for her poor mother.

When Louise had found her quietly sobbing, she was not only mourning Duncan, but was undoubtedly shocked at what the will had revealed to her. How lonely and lost she must have felt. As all these thoughts raced through Louise's mind, sleep finally interrupted and she had drifted off into another world.

On wakening the following morning, Louise had felt a pang of conscience. She felt it was wrong that she had read the will as it was her mother's property and, if it had caused emotional disturbances to her, it was all of her own doing. She got up, washed and dressed and, although she was feeling miserable, she forced herself to go into the kitchen for her breakfast, confident and smiling.

'Good morning, Mum. How about us getting down to business and sorting out what we are going to do for our summer holiday this year?' Louise felt so much compassion for her mother and she wanted to protect and comfort her but without letting on that she had read her father's will and, as a result, knew the inexpressible sadness that it must have caused her.

'A good idea, darling. I have been collecting a few brochures together, ranging from Cornwall, Scotland and Jersey to more adventurous, Mediterranean cruises!'

'Well, you say what you would like to do. After all is said and done, you have the unenviable task of paying for the holiday! I will only be able to pay when I leave college and start earning.'

'All right,' replied Mary. 'But it must be a joint decision, as it would be of no use if I chose a holiday that did not appeal to you as well as to myself.'

So the next hour was spent very happily as mother and daughter browsed through the various brochures and discussed the pros and cons of the different holidays on offer, but the one that came out on top was the cruise. A mixture of fun, travel, blue seas and sunshine – all the good life was there for the taking! It was agreed that this was the holiday for them and they intended to book it later in the day.

Somehow, Louise felt so much better when this decision had been made and felt it had given her mother something to look forward to – something new and exciting.

Louise knew that, for her mother's sake, she must act as if nothing had happened and that she had never read her father's will when temptation had got the better of her.

Chapter Two

This particular summer proved to be a mixture of fun, success and happiness for Louise, probably the last period in her life when she felt totally relaxed and carefree. The Mediterranean cruise was lovely for both mother and daughter alike.

The ship, the SS *Arcadia*, belonging to the P&O fleet, with a tonnage of 29,734 and a crew of seven hundred and eleven, had taken them deep into the Mediterranean waters. The destinations were all fascinating in their own ways. The *Arcadia* sailed from Southampton for a fifteen day journey and the passengers were given plenty of time to explore the ports of Palma, Split, Dubrovnik, Naples and Casablanca. Mary and Louise loved the whole experience of being on board a luxury liner and they very quickly made friends and entered into the shipboard way of life. It was a very reluctant mother and daughter who disembarked down the gangway after steaming a distance of 5,658 miles. Mary was sadder than Louise as she had loved the holiday so much that she shed quite a few tears when it came time to leave.

Louise was particularly pleased to see how her mother had entered into this completely different life with such enthusiasm and hoped that the whole holiday would refresh and strengthen her for the months ahead. They both had such a wonderful holiday. The day before sailing,

Louise had received her college diploma, listing all the qualifications she had achieved whilst on the course. She had done exceptionally well and so her next task after the vacation would be to apply for a job. This was exciting, if somewhat daunting for her, as this would be her first position. Louise was not in any hurry, but with the autumn only two months away, it would be nice to know that she was settled in a post.

Acquiring a job turned out to be easier and quicker than Louise imagined it would be! A few days after their return, the secretary from her college called and asked if she would be at all interested in working as a Personal Assistant to the owner of an art gallery in Cavendish Street. She explained that, when the vacancy came up, the owner of Maze Gallery had telephoned the college to see if a suitable candidate could be found as they had employed the last PA via the college. Louise had not thought of working in the art world; in fact, her inclinations had been to apply to work within the medical profession, probably due to being so close to her grandfather who was completely involved in all medical matters. However this position did appeal to her and she informed the secretary that she would willingly phone the gallery to make an appointment for an interview.

Mary, as always, encouraged her daughter to give of her best at the forthcoming interview and arranged to go with her to give her moral support. Louise appreciated this typically kind gesture of her mother's. As the interview was not until the afternoon, they had decided to go up to town in the morning in order to shop and to have a nice, leisurely lunch in Harrods. The Maze Gallery was only a stone's throw away from the store and so there would be no question of a need to worry about the time.

Louise's interview arrived and, after a relaxed morning

buying a birthday present for an ex-school friend, the two women had lunch at one of the restaurants in Harrods. At this point in time, Louise was becoming apprehensive and did not really do justice to the meal of poached salmon and new potatoes that the waitress had just served her. But Mary continued to chat away in her usual calm and soothing tone. Desserts, which usually Louise preferred to the main course, went by the board and she ordered a black coffee instead to calm her nerves.

The Maze Gallery presented a very impressive building. There were double doors, complete with gold-plate fittings, leading into a well-lit, large, square hall, fully carpeted and with large and beautifully framed pictures adorning the walls, with their own individual lights above to show them off to their best advantage. The first impression was good and rich, but certainly not flashy in any way. Louise felt comfortable and a feeling of confidence swept over her as she walked over to the lady sitting behind the reception desk.

'Good afternoon. I'm Louise Robson and I have come for an interview with Mr Peter Maze.'

'Right,' replied the receptionist with a welcoming smile. 'I will ring through to let him know you have arrived.'

With no more ado, she buzzed through to tell Mr Maze that Louise was there and was told to take her straight through to his office.

'Good luck, darling,' said Mary, who had been offered a chair beside the reception desk. 'I'll wait for you here.'

Louise was taken into an office on the ground floor, which was fairly small but the walls were covered with many pictures of all shapes and sizes with hardly a space between them. It was difficult to take it all in. A tall, slim man, with dark, wavy hair, which was greying at the temples, stood up from behind his desk and greeted Louise in a warm, easy fashion, with a firm handshake and a wide smile.

'Hello, Louise. I am Peter Maze. It is nice to meet you. Please, will you sit down.'

Louise sat in a large but comfortable, high-backed chair opposite him and prepared herself for her first interview.

Although Louise did not know a great deal about the art world, she found herself relaxed and at ease during the whole of the interview. She answered any questions that were put to her and her confidence grew by the minute. She also put in her fair share of questions to Mr Maze. He explained what her position at the gallery would entail and, at the end of her interview, Mr Maze offered Louise the job.

He then took Louise on a tour of the gallery after inviting Mary to join them. The gallery was situated on two floors and there were some beautiful pictures on show upstairs. The rooms there were for exhibition purposes, with two or three more offices tucked away at the end of a long corridor. Mr Maze explained that, should Louise decide to accept the position, one of these offices would become hers.

After the interview Louise and Mary had a great deal to talk about and they took themselves off to Fortnum and Mason for afternoon tea. This time Louise could really relax and indulge in a traditional English tea without having to worry about the interview.

During tea, Louise told her mother about her time with Peter Maze and what her job would involve. She also told her that she had decided to accept the position and that she would be starting by working a three-month probationary period. She had liked Peter and thought it would be a pleasure to work for him. Mary was pleased to listen to her daughter's enthusiastic account of her interview and said that, if she felt it was right for her, then certainly go ahead and accept, adding that she felt sure Louise would make a great success of anything that she chose to do and wished her all the luck in the world with it.

'By all means, go for it, Louise. I am more than confident that you will make a real go of anything you decide to do. You have a tremendous way of being able to 'give of yourself' and anyone that has ever been involved with you feels it. It is a great gift you have and your father had this same quality. He would be so proud of you, darling.'

Louise put her hand over her mother's and gave it a squeeze.

'Thank you for saying that. I want you to know that I am very proud to be your daughter. You have coped so well since Daddy died and I only wish he was here today to be part of our lives.'

No more was said, but mother and daughter's understanding of one another's feelings continued to grow.

Chapter Three

Louise settled into her routine at Peter's gallery. The days came and went and after working there three months Louise had become well and truly involved with all the gallery's dealings. She had got to know many of the artists who visited and who offered their paintings to Peter for sale.

Business was beginning to accelerate, because Christmas was approaching very fast. On a certain Wednesday morning at the beginning of December, an artist, by the name of Ralph Waters, entered the Maze Gallery and asked Louise if it was at all possible to see Peter with a view to holding an exhibition of his work.

Louise was not prepared for the effect that Ralph had on her; she was swept off her feet the minute his large, blue eyes penetrated hers. He had jet-black hair, which was swept back from his face and tied back into a ponytail. His face was young, enthusiastic and very animated. When he spoke, his face became alive and Louise thought she had never seen such incredible beauty in a man, even if he was somewhat Bohemian! She was fascinated by Ralph and his charm, which he used with every movement and every word he uttered. She was still staring at him when Peter walked across the hall towards them.

'Oh, Peter, I was just about to ring you, to see if it was possible for Mr Waters to come and see you regarding a showing of his work.'

'Fine, Louise, please take him into my office and I will be there in a couple of minutes after I have made a phone call.'

Louise asked Ralph to follow her and she showed him into Peter's office. A very odd feeling went through the whole of her body as she walked back to her own office. This was a feeling that she had never experienced before. It was a mixture of excitement and of apprehension.

She was so aware of his closeness she felt that she would like to have reached out and touched him. As she sat down at her desk she knew that there would be no chance of doing any further work whilst Ralph was still in Peter's office and so it came as a relief to her when the phone rang and Peter asked her to make him some coffee to share with his client.

As she arrived at the office carrying a tray of coffee she could feel her hands trembling at the thought of being in Ralph's presence.

'Thank you, Louise. Would you stay and write down some details of the forthcoming exhibition that I have agreed to put on at our gallery for Ralph.'

Louise literally felt her heart skip a beat. The sensation was extraordinary. The images of the paintings in her mind conjured up Ralph's work dominating the Maze Gallery, with him being the main artist. Her feeling was intense, a feeling of falling in love at first sight. She spent the rest of the afternoon in deep conversation with Ralph regarding the presentation of his work and the suitable days on which the exhibition should be held.

Louise learnt that Ralph had already distinguished himself in the art world. Now he needed to be recognised in London. By the end of the afternoon all the necessary details had been sorted out and a date had been fixed for the exhibition to go ahead shortly after Christmas. A date for an opening night was decided, when prospective purchasers would be invited to view Ralph's paintings and they would join him and the gallery staff for drinks and a buffet supper.

Louise felt intoxicated on her way home and she was unsure whether to discuss this meeting with Ralph to her mother or to wait and invite her to the opening night and introduce her to him then. She decided on the latter!

Christmas and New Year came and went, with Louise and her mother doing their usual round of visiting family and friends. Louise loved this time of giving and really was happier to give presents than to receive them. All through Christmas her thoughts were of Ralph and she longed for the forthcoming exhibition of his work. He had called into the gallery a few times to make final arrangements and Louise was always more than pleased to see him. She hoped that he felt the same way, but apart from always being friendly, he showed no signs of endearment towards her.

At about this time, Peter Maze began to show an interest in Louise, an interest that went far beyond those of a boss for his employee. It was Christmas time so it presented a good excuse for relationships to take off on a closer footing. Peter was at least twenty years older than Louise, but that certainly did not deter him from asking her out to dinner in the week before the Christmas activities went into full swing. Louise felt a mixed feeling of being flattered and fathered. She did accept his invitation and he took her to a lovely Italian restaurant in Knightsbridge for a meal. She ate her meal and chatted happily to Peter. A great deal of her conversation turned to Ralph's exhibition. In fact, she found it very difficult to keep off the subject of Ralph and had to stop herself from getting carried away and showing too much interest in him. At this stage, she did not want anyone, especially Peter, to guess what was going on in her mind.

After coffee and liqueurs, Peter offered to drive Louise home to Putney. His car was parked a few yards away from the restaurant and it gave Louise a warm, secure feeling to be escorted home rather than facing a journey back alone. Peter had a large, comfortable Bentley, certainly not the latest model, but it was only five years old and it was in immaculate condition. Louise sank back in the leather seat and looked forward to being driven back home in such a luxurious car.

As soon as they were seated in Peter's car, ready for the journey home, Peter stretched his left arm across Louise on the pretext of checking that her passenger door was firmly closed.

The events that were to take place next were entirely unexpected by Louise and were to leave her feeling nothing but contempt and utter distaste towards Peter, a man she had once admired.

Peter had his hand on the door handle when he made a grab for Louise's breast.

'Get off me, Peter!' Louise caught his hand and pushed it away from her body. Everything after that happened so quickly. Peter's face suddenly loomed up in front of hers as he crushed his lips forcefully on to Louise's mouth and she immediately felt his hot, wet tongue penetrate deep into her mouth, so much so that she almost started to gag on it. His hand was busy again going over the contours of her body. As he pressed hard on her, she sensed his hand working its way up her leg and a complete panic set in. Louise pushed him away with all her strength and almost spat out at him.

'Just get away from me and drive me home. Don't you

ever touch me or come near me like that again. In fact, stay away from me altogether. I am not, nor have I ever been, interested in you so just get that clear right here and now.'

Louise began to shake and was conscious of the tears that were now beginning to stream down her face. She was actually experiencing a fear of this man sitting next to her. Peter's face by now looked like thunder as he sat back into his seat.

Sarcastically, he said, 'Oh, come on, Louise. Don't act so innocent. I find it hard to believe that any girl would find a kiss and a fondle so terrible; most would welcome the attention that I am offering to you. You have enjoyed yourself this evening and I dare say you are well aware of my feelings towards you. I am certainly no saint and I hardly imagine you to be either.'

By now, Louise was sobbing uncontrollably and found it difficult to get any words out. She managed to snap back at him, with as much conviction as she could muster:

'That is not the point, Peter. I came out with you on the understanding of having a meal out, and you have blatantly taken advantage of me when I am stuck in your car. I want you to take me home right now or else I will make my own way home.'

'Fine, but don't expect any more favours from me in the future regarding anything, and that includes *his* work.'

With her words of rejection still resounding in his ears, Peter turned the engine on, put his car into gear and headed off towards Putney in complete silence.

Louise thankfully sat for the whole journey in silence as if frozen to the seat. She longed to be at home and rid of this man. She hated his uninvited sexual advances and she could feel her anger welling up inside. He had spoilt everything. The only man she desired to touch and to be touched by in return was Ralph. This man, Peter, who until now had treated her with respect, had repelled her more than she ever thought possible.

Peter's face gave nothing away as he drove steadily on towards Putney. When they reached her home she could not wait for the car to stop for her to get out. There was no repeat performance and, like the perfect gentleman, Peter got out of the car and went round the passenger side to open the door for Louise to get out. She got out, thanked Peter and literally ran to her front door without even a glance behind her. Peter made no attempt to follow her in and for this she was more than a little thankful.

After Louise had showered and got into bed, she lay there thinking of what had happened and continued to feel threatened and angry that Peter had behaved in such a way. The evening, until his advances, had gone so well, but the passion behind his attack was completely unnerving to her and from now on she knew that she would have to keep her distance from Peter Maze. The sad thing about the situation was that she loved her job and the thought of not being involved in Ralph's approaching exhibition was unbearable.

Chapter Four

The morning dawned and Louise lay in bed with her troubled thoughts going round and round in her young head. The evening had presented an odd picture to Louise; on the one hand she had thoroughly enjoyed her pasta meal and the well-chosen wine which had accompanied it and, on the other hand, the memory of Peter's unexpected attack had spoilt the entire evening.

It was not as if Peter was unattractive, in fact quite the reverse. Louise had quite often seen women making a play for his favours, without a great deal of success she had noticed. But he was definitely a lady's man and, although he had been married in his early twenties and divorced ten years later, he showed no signs of giving up his bachelor life! He lived in a penthouse just off Sloane Square. On the two occasions that Louise had visited his flat, once being with Peter's receptionist, when they were on their way to an exhibition at the Devonshire Club, and then another time, when she had had to pick up some sketches needed in the gallery when Peter was away in Brussels, Louise had found the flat beautifully decorated in the finest taste and furnished like a show flat. Peter certainly had style and it was reflected in his home. She wondered how many women he entertained in his pad, but imagined more that he wined and dined them at expensive restaurants and then maybe brought them home later to sample his coffee and his Napoleon Brandy. He could always take them home via his gallery if he wanted to show them his etchings!

Louise had always enjoyed working for Peter and loved the everyday running of the Maze Gallery, but she had always respected and liked Peter as a boss; she had never considered him in any other way. He had, in return, always shown her the utmost consideration and respect, as indeed he did to his other staff, and so what had happened the night before completely threw Louise's feelings into turmoil. Since her first meeting with Ralph Waters her thoughts had been entirely single-minded and he alone occupied all her romantic daydreams. Although it was obvious that Ralph was unaware of her intense feelings towards him, she thought she had somehow betrayed him by presenting a situation where Peter's passion could get the better of him.

This morning Louise did not have the same enthusiasm getting bathed and dressed, ready for work. This was unusual for her as each day presented a new challenge, which she normally enjoyed, but due to the previous night's occurrence, she felt embarrassed and exhausted, wondering where she would now stand in Peter's eyes.

This morning she felt worried and a deep feeling of apprehension flooded over her. Peter had virtually ignored her during the drive back to Putney; it was as if his moment of unwanted passion had never taken place.

Louise could not get it out of her mind and wondered if Peter was aware this morning of what had really happened the previous night. He could not have forgotten. Did he make a habit of pouncing on his lady guests in that manner or had it been a one-off situation? She could hardly pluck up the courage to ask him. It just all seemed so strange to Louise. She had been kissed by boys before, but this was different. Peter was her boss and old enough to be her father.

She arrived at the gallery cold and tired. The weather had taken a downward spiral and it was degrees colder. People were dressed for warmth, with their coats and scarves wrapped tightly around them to keep out the bitter December winds. As she walked through the hall, Peter was talking to the receptionist and looked up when Louise approached them.

'Good morning, Louise. I hope you are not chilled to the marrow as it is so much colder than yesterday.'

'No, I am fine thank you, but I am looking forward to a cup of coffee to get me in gear.'

With these short and sweet greetings, Louise made her way to her office and plugged in the kettle for her coffee. Within a few minutes, Peter appeared in her doorway.

'I hope you enjoyed our meal as much as I did, Louise. I feel a little embarrassed, but I do apologise if you were offended by my passion but I have wanted to do that for a long time. I know you are very young, but I do find you very attractive and desirable and my feelings as a man just got the better of me.'

Then, without another word, Peter turned around and left Louise alone in her office. She was not given the chance to reply to his statement even if she had wanted to. She thought that it was to his credit that he had at least had the decency and manners to apologise to her instead of just ignoring it and he immediately went up in her estimation. Louise made her coffee and drank it down straight away and it made her feel a great deal better able to cope with the day's work.

With the interruption of Christmas and New Year, it seemed endless waiting for Ralph's exhibition to start, which was scheduled for Monday, 14th January. After New Year, Ralph called into the gallery daily, bringing his paintings to hang on display. The opening night came at last and about one hundred special guests had been invited along to enjoy Ralph's preview and to sample an excellent cold buffet supper with a selection of carefully chosen wines. Peter Maze opened the exhibition and gave a welcoming speech, which included much praise for Ralph's work.

Louise had bought a lovely black dress for this very special evening. It was soft wool which clung to her slim figure. She wore very little make-up and her hair shone in the electric lighting. She looked really pretty and collected many admiring glances. She worked hard, making sure that everyone had drinks in their hands and that they had been given a catalogue containing all of the works in Ralph's display. She was very happy that her mother was there and she made quite sure that she introduced her to Ralph. Most of the time, when she had a chance to talk to Mary, she was talking intensely to Peter. The thought crossed her mind to wonder what her mother would think of him if she knew of his passionate kiss and grope of her daughter? But tonight, Louise was overjoyed at being part of what was going on for Ralph and she could barely take her eyes off him.

At one stage, she was sure that he had given her a lingering, meaningful look; it could have been her imagination, but the feeling made her warm inside.

The evening was an enormous success with many of Ralph's pieces of art being purchased. He was so thrilled and he talked incessantly to all around him. At the end, he gave a short speech to thank all the people for coming and made a special thank you to Peter and his staff for making his exhibition all possible. Louise felt ten feet tall and almost took the thank you as if it had been directed just at her. Before she went home with her mother, Ralph came up to Louise and put a hand on each of her shoulders and bent down to give her a kiss on both cheeks.

'Thanks, Louise, you are a very special young lady and you have contributed so much to the success of my exhibition.'

'Well, it was a team effort, Ralph, and we all found it a pleasure to work with you,' Louise replied. She had never felt so elated in her life, as she had been when he had touched her, a feeling totally opposite to the way she had felt when Peter had touched her.

Chapter Five

Ralph's background and training in art was carried out at an Academy. He had done exceptionally well at school and art had always been his most important subject. From there he had gone on to achieve his ambition, to become an artist, specialising in landscapes. From quite a young boy he was interested in the fine arts and in the study of the history of art. He had never ever considered any other career. He was a gentle man, his manners were courteous and he dressed in typical artist's fashion, very colourful and casual, with bright orange, purple or red shirts, a cravat instead of a tie and light-coloured trousers or jeans being the order of the day. He looked every inch the artist!

Ralph's work consisted mainly of landscapes and seascapes. His favourite artist was John Constable and his studio was lined with bookshelves bearing Constable's works and a great deal of other literature about him.

Ralph had visited and painted in Suffolk, which was a source of inspiration and beauty to him. He felt the presence of Constable was still there and, as for Constable, the countryside proved to be a place of delight to the young artist. Also, like Constable did in 1799, Ralph attended the Royal Academy School in London. The English painters who most influenced his work were Richard Wilson, Turner, Gainsborough, but above all, John Constable.

When Louise arrived at the gallery on the morning after

the evening preview of Ralph's exhibition, she found a note written in Ralph's handwriting on her desk. It was very simple and to the point:

'Many thanks again, Louise, for all your help and support. Please meet me at eight o'clock at the main entrance of Harrods and I will take you for a drink!' It was signed, 'Ralph'.

Nothing more and nothing less! Louise just sat there in a daze – it was the most wonderful note she had ever received! She just could not believe that Ralph wanted to see her on her own and she almost felt dizzy with anticipation. She telephoned her mother to say that she would not be in for a meal, but would be home at eleven o'clock at the latest. She knew how Mary would worry if Louise did not give her some indication of a time.

The day dragged and Louise thought the evening would never come; probably a second did not pass without her thinking about Ralph. She experienced a longing for him that almost frightened her. She imagined that Peter had experienced similar feelings for her and a wave of pity for him swept through her. If she had felt the same it would have been so easy, but life was not like that.

Although Peter was still very charming towards her, Louise sensed a change in him. It was the way she caught him watching her and the easy rapport, which had been between them, had become slightly strained.

At about three o'clock Peter came into Louise's office to discuss Ralph's opening night.

'It certainly went well, Louise, and the Press intend to give him all the credit that he is due. Ralph has worked very hard and he deserves to achieve success and I would like to thank you for all you did to contribute to making the evening go so well.'

'It was a pleasure and an honour to be part of it all,' replied Louise. She felt so proud of Ralph and hoped that her enthusiasm did not show too much to Peter. They continued to discuss the exhibition for a while and then Peter said:

'Louise, how about I take you out for a meal this evening, just a little celebration for the two of us? I know you liked that Italian meal we had last time and I would very much like to repeat it, so tonight would be great.'

Louise almost froze at the thought of dinner alone with Peter.

'I really am sorry, Peter, but I already have a prior engagement for tonight.'

'Not to worry, Louise, we will make it some other time. I should have realised that an attractive young lady like you would be in big demand. But I would still like to think that I stand a chance to wine and dine you. We will take a rain check on it.'

With those words, he went out of her office, closing the door quietly behind him.

Louise felt uncomfortable when he had gone. There was something about Peter, the way he looked and spoke towards her. He was trying so hard to be natural, but it was not coming across too well and Louise felt uneasy. She had chosen not to say that she was going out with Ralph because she sensed that Peter would not take kindly to hearing this piece of news. Also she did not want to give him the slightest indication of just how smitten she was by Ralph. Somehow, she did not understand why Peter had, but he had taken the edge off her longing to see Ralph.

A few minutes later, Peter appeared again in the doorway to her office and said, 'By the way, Louise, I have just come off the phone to your mother. I asked her if I could take *her* out for a drink this evening and she agreed and so I shall be driving out to Putney to collect her and then I intend to take her to a little pub I know of, called The Fox and Grapes on Wimbledon Common. It is a pity you will not be able to join us, but hopefully I might see you later.'

With that, he turned around and was gone.

Louise felt a mixture of anger and resentment. Peter has asked her mother out in order to get back at Louise for turning his invitation down and she felt it was grossly unfair. Peter would be an ideal suitor for her mother in the ordinary way, but she did not want her to be used by him.

Eight o'clock did come round at last and, when Louise arrived at the main entrance to Harrods, Ralph was waiting for her. She could feel herself flushing with excitement and he seemed genuinely pleased to see her. He gave her a quick hug and a peck on each cheek and then tucked his arm through hers quite naturally and off they set.

'I know a wine bar just around the corner and we can get a snack there as well. One thing about Knightsbridge, we are spoilt for choice of places to eat and drink; it's a wonder they all manage to stay in business with such competition!'

Ralph talked so easily and Louise loved it. As a result she found it easy and very natural to be with him. It was as if she had always known him.

Once in the wine bar, several people acknowledged Ralph and a couple came over and talked to him at their table. Not for long, but long enough for Louise to wish they would go away! She wanted Ralph all to herself and she regarded every minute as precious. She literally hung on his every word.

The evening went by very quickly and then it was time for Louise to make her way home. Ralph did offer to accompany her, but Louise said that as he lived in the completely opposite direction he must go his way and she would take the underground to Earl's Court, and then the District Line to Putney Bridge. From there she caught the number eighty-five bus which took her right to her door. This was the journey that she did every day to and from the gallery and it did not worry her in the slightest. Ralph, on the other hand, had a studio on the outskirts of Hampstead and so their journeys bore no resemblance in direction whatsoever.

Ralph walked with Louise to the tube and, on parting, put both his arms around her and held her close. She just melted and stayed there until he held her away from him and then he said,

'Goodnight, Louise, it has been great seeing you on your own and I would like to do it again. Next time you must come to my studio and I will cook you some supper in my humble abode.'

Then he gave Louise a quick kiss and ran off in the direction of his platform.

When Louise arrived home, it was to her utter dismay that she saw Peter's car parked outside her home. She had been so preoccupied in daydreaming about Ralph, that she had not even given a thought to Peter and her mother. Now she remembered that Peter had told her of his evening date with Mary. She put her key in the front door and was met in the hall by Peter and her mother. Apparently Peter was just about to take his leave.

'Hello, Louise, I hoped that I would see you before I left for home. Mary and I have spent a really nice evening at this little pub on Wimbledon Common and we both agreed that you would enjoy the atmosphere in there. They also do evening meals and so I have booked for the three of us to have dinner there next Tuesday. I hope this arrangement meets with your approval.'

Louise noted that, in his enthusiasm to tell her about next Tuesday, he had not even asked her if she had spent a good evening, added to which he had obviously assumed that she would be free to go out with them next Tuesday. She resented the fact that it had been arranged without first consulting her and she felt like saying something to that effect. However, she resisted the temptation, remembering that Peter was, after all was said and done, her boss. She knew by the way Peter looked at her that he still had designs on her and that he was definitely using her mother to achieve his own ends.

What had been a lovely, happy evening to her was now being spoilt by Peter's presence in her own home and she was somewhat relieved when he finally left.

'Did you have a good evening, darling?' asked Mary.

'Great,' replied Louise. 'Ralph took me to this really busy wine bar in Knightsbridge, called The Wine and Cork, where nearly every other person in there seemed to know Ralph! My only complaint was that the evening went by far too quickly!'

'Tell me to mind my own business, darling, but I detect that you are very smitten with Ralph and, believe me, it shows! Even Peter commented on it during the course of the evening and I got the distinct impression that he did not like it one little bit.'

'It certainly is my business, Mother, and Peter has no right to either approve or disapprove of with whom I choose to spend my evening. What I do after working hours is entirely up to me and the sooner Peter accepts that fact, the better.'

'The trouble is', replied Mary, 'that Peter has quite

obviously fallen for you and therefore is resentful of Ralph and your adoration for him. Actually, as it turned out, Peter spent most of this evening questioning me about you, which, as you can imagine, did not go down too well with me! When he realised that I did not like his probing, he changed the subject. Also, I could not stop him from booking the dinner date for next Tuesday evening. It did put me in an awkward position because, at the end of the day, you do work for him!'

'I know,' sighed Louise. 'It is grossly unfair on you for him to put you in this position. Never mind, we will go on Tuesday, but at the same time we will make it clear that we do not intend to make a habit of dining out with him!'

Louise looked affectionately at Mary. It was good to have a mother who was her best friend as well as being her mother, someone with whom Louise could talk openly. She could feel the warmth and the closeness between them. Louise wondered then how much Mary was still missing Duncan and how much of the past was troubling her.

Chapter Six

Louise had slept well despite going to bed with a troubled mind. After all, she was not answerable to Peter Maze and just because she worked for him certainly he did not own her.

She woke up early, at about half past five and was surprised at how refreshed she felt. Her thoughts returned quickly to the events of the night before and she felt stronger with her approach towards the new day. How dare Peter use her mother to get through to her? It was all so obvious that this Tuesday dinner date had been contrived in order to have an evening out with herself. Her mother was just a pawn in Peter's scheme and she had had to be included to make sure that Louise would attend the evening. It was so clear and it irritated Louise more and more.

She should be free now to concentrate on Ralph. Louise knew that he was the man she wanted and who she felt sure was attracted to her. She had felt the vibrations last evening and they were good. If it had not been for the episode with Peter, Louise would have gone to bed just thinking about Ralph. He was really someone special to her. He had awakened all the longings in Louise's young body and she sometimes felt dizzy with her desire for him. She knew without a doubt that, given the right opportunity, she would surrender herself to him. In fact, she longed and dreamed for it to happen and, in her heart, she knew that it was just a question of time until it did. She was too young and inexperienced to separate desire and love. Desire at this stage was probably the true feelings she felt, but no doubt love would grow as she got to know him more intimately.

Louise saw Peter Maze as a big problem and she did not quite know how to tackle it. She had no desire towards Peter. She liked him and, to some extent, she respected him, but she neither loved nor wanted him. He had now become a threat to her, particularly to her peace of mind. She wanted to be free to concentrate her feelings entirely on Ralph, but Peter made this impossible.

Her mood as she travelled to the gallery was apprehensive, to say the least. She shut the office door behind her, but it was very quickly opened again by Peter.

'Good morning, Louise,' he said. 'I received an early call from Ralph and he is calling into the gallery at lunchtime to bring five or six more paintings to add to his show. I have a prior lunch appointment and so I wonder if you would arrange to hang his pictures where you think fit.'

'Of course I will, Peter. Leave it to me. I will probably have quite a job squeezing them in, but I will try to find spaces for them.'

'Thank you, Louise. I knew I could rely on you.' With these words, Peter took his leave.

Louise's heartbeat hastened. Ralph was coming in to the gallery at lunchtime and she would virtually have him to herself!

The morning dragged on and Louise got through her work quicker than usual; it was as if she was running a race towards lunchtime! She did not want to lose any precious time doing her work when she could be spending time with Ralph.

At precisely one o'clock there was a knock on her office door and in swept Ralph carrying his pictures under both arms. She had never seen him looking so suave and she had a tremendous urge to embrace him. She had to use all her powers of self-control to stop her womanly desires. She had heard of women having hot flushes, but she was experiencing one well before her time! Ralph, on the other hand, presented himself as a young man who was cool, calm and collected.

'The receptionist told me to come along to your office as Peter has gone out to lunch. She said that you would be kind enough to hang my pictures for me.'

'Right,' said Louise. 'I'm ready when you are. Would you like a drink before we go?'

'Thank you for offering, but I am in quite a hurry as I have an appointment in Piccadilly with a fellow artist at half past two, so I will have to make this visit short and sweet. However, while I am here, how about you and me making a date for supper as soon as it is convenient for you.'

Louise's first reaction was to arrange the date for after next Tuesday evening. By then dinner with Peter and her mother would be over. She felt instinctively that she would need Ralph to confide in, if she thought it necessary.

'If it would suit you, Ralph, I could make either Wednesday or Thursday evening of next week. I am free on both those evenings.'

Ralph replied, 'That will be fine. Let's make it Wednesday at my studio at seven o'clock. I will give you directions on how to get there before I leave.'

They then went to the exhibition hall to decide where to hang Ralph's new paintings. As Louise and Ralph were walking along the landing on their way to the exhibition gallery, an attractive lady, with dark, wavy hair, which was beginning to go slightly grey and enormous blue eyes, approached them.

'I am sorry to bother you, but I think that the gallery's receptionist must be somewhere else in the building. I wonder if you would be kind enough to direct me to the exhibition currently being shown by Ralph Waters?'

'Of course,' replied Louise. 'Come along with us. We are just on our way to hang some more paintings of Ralph's. By the way, this is Ralph Waters himself and I am Louise. I work here for Peter Maze, the owner of the gallery.'

'Oh, thank you. I will follow you. What an added bonus to meet you in person, Mr Waters; I so admire your work.'

They arrived in the exhibition hall and Louise gave the visitor a catalogue and then proceeded to discuss with Ralph where they could put his additional paintings. At the same time Louise could not help being aware of a feeling of loneliness which radiated from this lady who was by now occupied in viewing Ralph's work. Louise noted how intensely she studied each and every picture, referring all the time to the catalogue.

The pictures were duly hung and it was now time for Ralph to take his leave and go on to his appointment in Piccadilly.

'Thank you, Louise. As always, you have been a great help. I will see you before next Wednesday and give you the directions to my studio.' With those words, Ralph gave her a quick kiss on her cheek and he was gone.

The lady visitor looked up. 'How nice for me to view the artist as well as his works. I certainly got my timing right!'

Louise felt instantly drawn to this figure and experienced a strange feeling that she knew her from somewhere; she recognised her face but could not think where they had previously met.

'Yes,' replied Louise. 'Ralph had just called in for a few minutes to deliver six extra paintings. His exhibition is going well and we think that most of his pictures will sell. Landscapes and seascapes are still very much in demand and, as you will see, some of them have already got RESERVED on them. His preview was very successful and he has also been commissioned to paint for a buyer who lives on the West Coast of Scotland. I understand that the scenery up there is unbelievably beautiful and Ralph will have the sea and the countryside to work on.'

It suddenly hit Louise where she had first seen this visitor. It was the lone figure that she had seen at her father's funeral. Louise felt hot and sick, but she knew she must continue to act normally so as to give nothing away of her identity.

They chatted on for a while about the paintings and then Louise said, 'I am going to make a cup of coffee for myself. Can I do one for you at the same time?'

The lady replied, 'That would be lovely. I would just like to choose a picture as it is my brother's birthday next week. He has just moved home and there is a large wall in his dining room which is just crying out for one of these paintings!'

'I will go and make the coffee and then come back to collect you. Please take your time, and I will see you when you are ready.'

'I already know which one I am going to purchase. It is this one.' The lady pointed to a seascape which Ralph had painted in Sussex. It was of Beachy Head, at Eastbourne, with the sea crashing against the lighthouse and on to the rocks which surround it.

Louise liked the picture and it was one of her favourites. She could almost feel the fury of the sea as Ralph had captured it hitting the rocks with such force.

Louise gave the visitor another twenty minutes to study all of Ralph's works. She then went along to collect her and to take her to her office for coffee.

'Hello again, Louise. I have definitely decided on the Beachy Head picture, so please would you put a reserve on it and we will complete the deal with the required deposit.'

'Certainly,' replied Louise. 'Please come into my office and we can sort out the necessary details.'

Louise poured them each a cup of coffee and her visitor got her cheque book out to write the required deposit.

'Do I make my cheque out to the gallery or to Ralph Waters himself?'

'To the gallery, please. At the end of the exhibition we will pay Ralph for all the pictures that we have sold for him and, of course, the gallery takes the commission that is due!'

Louise was finding this lady so very easy to talk to. She looked at the cheque as it was handed to her and, when she read the signature, her heart almost missed a beat. It was signed Anne Robson. Louise's pulse raced and for a minute she held on tight to the edge of her desk before saying:

'Thank you, Mrs Robson. I will go right away and put a reserved label on your picture and, if you will give me your telephone number, I will call you when the picture is ready for you to collect.'

When Mrs Robson had left, thoughts came painfully into Louise's mind. She had just met her father's common-law wife. His will had involved this lady with whom Louise had just had coffee and an easy chat and to whom she had sold one of Ralph's paintings. This meeting was a chance in a million and Louise felt an inexpressible warmth towards her. She felt she knew her through her father. She wanted to run after her and ask her to come back and continue to talk to her, but instead, she froze.

Perhaps it was the easy way out, even the coward's way out, but Louise decided there and then that she did not want to meet Anne again nor to delve into her father's past. What had happened in those far-off days was their affair and had nothing to do with Louise, either then or now. She wanted just to remember her father as she had known him. She knew that that was how he would have wanted it.

Louise would arrange for another member of Peter's staff to telephone Anne to collect her painting when Ralph's exhibition had finished. There was nothing to be gained in raking up the past.

Her mother never had and Louise had always respected and loved her for this.

Chapter Seven

Tuesday arrived and with it the prospect of dinner in the evening with Peter. Louise had firmly decided that Peter would not be allowed to make these arrangements for her ever again and she had every intention of telling him so if the opportunity presented itself.

It did, in fact, prove to be a pleasant evening with a good meal at Peter's chosen little pub on Wimbledon Common. Louise had mixed feelings because it was quite obvious to her that her mother was thoroughly enjoying herself and the conversation and laughter flowed easily between all three of them.

Louise's thoughts, however, were constantly of Ralph and she was so looking forward to seeing him again the next evening as they had arranged. His name came into the conversation on several occasions, and Louise did notice a change in Peter's voice whenever Ralph's name was mentioned. In fact, there was a distinct coolness bordering on sarcasm, as if he wanted to belittle him in Louise's presence.

As the three of them drove home, Louise looked intently at her mother and thought how concerned she would be if she knew that Anne Robson had bought one of Ralph's paintings earlier that day. She also felt how easy life would be if Peter would wine and dine Mary and not include her.

When Peter took his leave of them he said, 'Thank you, ladies. It was great having your company. I shall certainly invite you to join me again for an evening.' And, with that, he took his leave of them and drove off back into town.

'I did enjoy myself,' said Mary. 'I hope you did, Louise despite you not really wanting to be there!'

'Yes, Mother, I did, but I still feel uneasy in Peter's company and wish he just kept me on a business level. I do not want anything else from him and I am certainly not going to let him make a habit of inviting me out. It makes me feel guilty to take his hospitality when really I do not want it.' Louise added, 'I shall be out tomorrow evening, but this time it will be with Ralph and I know I can tell you that that is where my heart is.'

'I realise that, darling,' replied Mary, 'but be careful as artists are a special breed and I would not like to see you get hurt.'

Louise felt full of compassion. Her poor mother had been betrayed and hurt by her husband and would now dread any emotional turmoil in her daughter's life.

The studio where Ralph lived and worked was on the fringe of Camden Lock and the Regent's Canal glided peacefully nearby. Louise thought how romantic it would be in the summer to go on a trip with Ralph along the canal to Little Venice and to visit the market at Camden Lock and even go on to London Zoo. Come to think of it, she really would not mind where she was as long as it was with Ralph!

His studio was at the top of a three-storeyed house and it had a large window in the roof which let in a great deal of light. It had originally been designed as a studio and the rest of the rooms in the house were let out to students and people who needed to work in this area. Ralph explained to Louise that an uncle of his owned the house and he had let Ralph live and work there for the past five years at a very reasonable rate. The studio was full of paintings, canvases, all at various stages, easels, paints, brushes and so on and the whole room gave Louise a warm, contented feeling. Here was Ralph's domain where he worked hard to make his living. He also showed Louise the rest of his rooms. They comprised a very small kitchen, with just the bare essentials in it and an equally small bathroom, which consisted of a shower, toilet and a washbasin. The only other room was where he slept and which doubled as a living room. It had a bed, a two-seater settee, a small television and a card table propped up against the wall with two folding chairs.

'This is where I eat and sleep, Louise! Nothing at all glamorous about it, but it is my home and I love every inch of it! It also suits me because I can concentrate on my work and that is what I like doing best. Now I am going to ask you to sit down while I cook us some supper.'

Ralph gave Louise a magazine and settled her comfortably on to the settee. He put the card table up with the two chairs and produced a tablecloth, which he threw over the table. He then laid it with various knives and forks and in the centre placed a candle, which he lit. By the time he had finished, the table looked attractive and the glow of the candle added a warm atmosphere to the whole room. Louise looked at the magazine, which Ralph had left with her while he had gone to prepare their supper, but she certainly was not able to concentrate on what she was looking at. She thought how very independent Ralph was and how touched she felt that he had invited her into his home so that he could share it with her. It was a sign to Louise that he wanted her to be part of his life.

Ralph came in to put a salad and bread rolls on the table. 'By the way, Louise, did that lady buy one of my paintings? You know, the one who came in while I was hanging my last six.'

'Yes, she reserved your Beachy Head one. She so admired your work and was buying it for her brother's birthday present.'

'Good news,' answered Ralph. 'I thought she was very charming – not, I might add, because she has purchased one of my paintings – but she seemed such a soft, vulnerable lady.'

'I agree,' said Louise. 'She was gentle, but she also knew what she wanted.'

Louise decided at this stage not to divulge all she really knew about Mrs Robson. It was best that Ralph just thought of her as another purchaser.

Ralph went back into his kitchen and called 'Take your seat, Louise; the food is on its way!' He duly appeared with a steaming dish of spaghetti Bolognese and a bottle of red wine. 'I know you like Italian food, Louise, and, come to mention it, this is all we've got!'

Louise assured Ralph that Italian was her favourite and they proceeded to eat. The meal was delicious and Ralph had chosen a claret to drink which complemented the Bolognese. The dessert was ice cream and fruit cocktail and neither of them could tackle the cheese which Ralph offered her. Afterwards, Louise helped wash up and sat down on the settee. Ralph put on a tape for background music; it was a selection of James Last. It was playing quietly, but certainly loud enough to be heard. They chatted together very comfortably about nothing in particular, but with the ease of two people who felt very relaxed in one another's company. The evening just raced by and Louise said that it was time to go as she did not want her mother worrying about her.

'My mother has had enough worries to last her a lifetime, Ralph, and I do not want to add to them. I guess it has not been an easy task to cope single-handed with a daughter and all the caring that goes along with it.'

'Of course, Louise. I certainly know by now how much your mother means to you and you have got quite a journey back home from here. Please phone me when you get home or else you will have me worrying about your safety as well!'

With these words from Ralph, Louise felt very warm inside and she knew beyond a doubt that her feelings were returned. When she got to the door she turned round quite naturally and put her arms around Ralph's neck and waited for him to kiss her. He bent down and gave her a lingering kiss. She felt his body pressing hard against hers, pulling her as close as he could. To Louise this felt so right; she loved this young artist and she was not afraid to express her feelings. She drew away.

'Ralph, I must go now but I will phone you when I get home to let you know that all is well.'

'All right, darling, I really don't want to let you go, but I know you must and maybe I would not be able to control my feelings if you stayed. Tomorrow, we will go out somewhere in the evening.' Ralph bent down and gave her another long and tender kiss.

Louise travelled home with her mind in a whirl. There was Ralph, Peter and now Anne Robson all mixed up in her thoughts. She wondered whether to have a heart-to-heart with her mother on her return, but thought better of it; instead she kept her feelings to herself.

Desire was a feeling she had never experienced before. She wanted Ralph and her young body was more than ready for him.

On her return home she duly phoned Ralph to let him know that she had travelled home in just over an hour and that she was now safe and sound. He sounded so tender and again she wanted him with every fibre in her body.

When she arrived at the gallery the next morning, Peter was waiting for her in her office.

'Good morning, Louise. I have been waiting here to invite you to be my hostess this evening at my club in order to entertain another gallery owner and his wife. I thought a really good dinner followed by coffee and brandy would put him in the right mood to show some of our pictures that are becoming somewhat hard to sell. How does the idea appeal to you, my dear?'

Louise's heart sank. She did not want to spend an evening with Peter, whether it was for business or for pleasure. Her mind reacted very quickly. 'I'm sorry, Peter, but tonight is out of the question. I am already having dinner with a friend whom I was at college with.' Louise found herself lying quite easily to him.

'Not to worry. I shall go and phone your mother and ask her to be my hostess instead. If I cannot have one of the beautiful Robson ladies, I shall have to try the other!'

With that, he swept out of her office and left Louise feeling awkward and angry. Once again Peter was going to use her mother. Also, her mother was bound to be questioned by Peter as to where Louise had gone this evening. She felt a tremendous desire to phone Ralph to get it off her chest to him, but at the same time she needed to think it through carefully. After all, it could be quite genuine that he needed a hostess and Louise was part of his gallery staff.

The rest of the day went by very slowly. Her mother had called to say that she would not be in this evening as she was coming up to town to meet Peter at his club for dinner. Louise just stopped herself from saying yes I know, he had already asked her and she had refused. Instead Louise wished her mother a happy evening and said that she would see her at breakfast the next day. Already she felt Peter was making it difficult for her to be as honest as she had always been.

After lunch her telephone rang and to her delight it was Ralph on the other end. 'Louise, I have managed to get two tickets for a concert at the Royal Albert Hall this evening. Will you come with me?'

'Need you ask? Of course I would love to come with you, Ralph. Where and what time shall I meet you?'

Ralph told her about a little Italian restaurant called Dino's at South Kensington opposite the tube station, and arranged to meet her there at six o'clock.

Louise replaced the receiver and turned around to go. In the doorway stood Peter, who was just staring at her. 'I never realised that it was Ralph who was the old college friend. Well, have a good evening, my dear.'

To her horror Louise realised that Peter had been standing there listening to her call and he would now know that she had lied to him that morning. She felt a wave of guilt pass over her and she had to pull herself together very quickly.

What was happening with Peter was taking away all the pleasure from her romance with Ralph and she felt that, when the opportunity arose, she would have to tell Ralph what a difficult situation Peter was creating between herself, her mother and her feelings towards him.

A few short months ago, Louise had been happy and relaxed and had really enjoyed coming to work each day to the gallery, but now it was all being spoilt by Peter, who was casting a shadow over her life.

Chapter Eight

The evening loomed up and Louise made quite sure that she was at Dino's restaurant by six o'clock. Ralph was already in there and was sipping a glass of red wine while studying the menu. He rose when he saw her enter.

'Hello, darling. Have you had a good day?'

'Not really, Ralph. I'm not enjoying working at the gallery as much as I used to.'

She felt an urge to burst into tears, but very quickly took control of her emotions. Louise was a proud person and she certainly would not want to make a public exhibition of herself.

'Please tell me what's wrong, Louise,' Ralph enquired kindly and then ordered a drink for her and also a portion of lasagne with some French bread.

'Well, it sounds ridiculous, but Peter is making me feel so uncomfortable and I really don't know how much longer I can continue to work for him.'

'I had a feeling that was at the root of it. As a matter of fact, he telephoned me today at my studio and more or less implied that he would not be requiring my paintings at his gallery again. I sensed by the tone of his voice that he was really annoyed, even angry, about something. But then he is quite a powerful man in the art world and he could certainly 'make or break' a young artist such as the likes of myself. I just don't understand what has made him like this.

We always used to have a very good working relationship.'

Louise decided to tell Ralph the truth. 'It's because of me. I know this is being disloyal to my boss, but he has been making passes at me for the last few months. He has even involved my mother to try to achieve this end. Tonight he asked me to be his hostess at a dinner and because I said 'No' he telephoned my mother, who, I believe, has quite a soft spot for him, and invited her instead. To make it all worse, he overheard me talking to you on the phone when you invited me out this evening. To my shame, I had already told him a white lie by saying I was spending the evening with an old college friend.'

Ralph thought for a while before answering, 'Of course. It all makes sense now and that explains why he telephoned me. To say he would not be requiring my paintings for any further exhibitions was really a threat made in his moment of anger.'

Louise replied, 'I always knew that you did not mix business with pleasure, but Peter obviously thinks otherwise.'

They continued to chat together and, despite Louise's problems, they enjoyed their meal and Louise felt a great deal better for sharing her anxiety with Ralph. She found him so easy to talk to and she could feel herself completely relaxing in his company.

After the meal, they walked arm in arm up to the Albert Hall where they enjoyed a concert given by Gilbert O'Sullivan, plus a full supporting cast. It turned out to be a happy evening and Ralph held her hand gently throughout the concert. Louise knew she was in love with this man and only hoped that he felt the same way about her.

As they were coming down the steps of the Royal Albert Hall, Ralph said, 'I will have to think seriously about getting myself a set of wheels. I just don't like the thought of you having to travel back alone to one side of London while I go off to the other and all by public transport.'

'Don't worry about me, Ralph. It really is not a bad journey and I'm quite used to it by now.'

'The other suggestion would be that you came to live with me at my studio. I am quite sure you know by now how I feel about you, Louise, even though it is early days yet.'

'Yes, Ralph, but I am not ready for that commitment. I do feel very strongly for you and I will know when the time is right. I do appreciate you asking me, but for the time being, I would like to get to know you better. Also, I am so unsettled in my mind regarding my job, Peter Maze and my mother.'

Ralph put his arms reassuringly around her and took her to South Kensington underground station.

He kissed her goodbye and whispered, 'I understand, darling, and you are not to worry. I love you very much and I cannot bear the thought of you being so troubled.'

When Louise arrived home, her mother was in the kitchen making a cup of coffee. 'Did you have a good evening?' Mary asked her daughter.

'Yes, lovely, thank you. I went to a little Italian restaurant in South Kensington and then on to a Gilbert O'Sullivan concert at the Albert Hall with Ralph.'

'Funny you didn't mention it to me when I phoned you this morning, Louise, but I am glad you had a good time.'

'Did you enjoy your evening, Mother?'

'Yes, it was very pleasant. Peter took me to his club where we met another gallery owner and his wife and we had dinner and drinks and then Peter talked business over their brandies, whilst I talked away with Mr Owen's wife,

Gwen, who was good company. Actually, you have only just missed Peter by about five minutes. I got the impression from him that you said to him that you had gone out with an old friend from college, but I said you hadn't mentioned it to me as I thought you were at home this evening.'

Louise thought she detected a note of sarcasm in her mother's voice, but she chose to ignore it. She was tired and wanted to go to bed, not to sleep, but to do some serious thinking.

Louise tossed and turned. She did not feel that Peter had the right to make her feel uncomfortable over her relationship with Ralph. It was nothing to do with him who she went out with. He was also making her feel uncomfortable with her mother, almost as if he was playing one against the other. Her mother was the last person she would ever want to hurt. She was everything to Louise and she had had a very close and loving relationship with her. It was extraordinary that in such a short space of time, Peter Maze had become so dominant in her life. When going through the order papers with Louise, he had even made a remark about the deposit cheque paid by Mrs Anne Robson. 'How odd, Louise. She has got the same surname as you. Is she any relation of yours?'

Very quickly, Louise had given a sharp 'No'. It only needed Peter to pass this information on to her mother to stir up another hornet's nest. What a pity that Anne Robson had decided to visit Peter's gallery out of all the art galleries there were in London.

It had been strange to actually have met the lady whom her father had loved so passionately. There would have been many questions she would have loved to have asked her about her father, but it was best left alone.

Ralph then came back into her mind. She really was besotted with him. She just accepted him for who he was and she realised that she had not even questioned him about his past. That really did not matter; what mattered was that she loved him for who he was now. He was so different from any other boy or man she had ever met before. He was unusual; he stood out in a crowd, even if it was because of the way he dressed with his bright, flamboyant colours! He was such a warm character, both in his dress and his manner. She knew she loved him and was happy that he had even suggested that they should share a home together. But maybe it was because of her mother or because of her fear of making a mistake that she refused. Also she felt she was answerable to Peter Maze, but she did not really know why he should even come into this situation at all. She still respected him as her boss, but her respect was also mingled with fear. He had the power to interfere with her two closest relationships, the one with her mother and the one with Ralph. He gave the impression that he was the sort of man who usually got what he wanted. But she was determined that he was not going to get her.

Eventually Louise drifted off into a restless sleep. In the morning she was woken by her alarm clock and she got up and showered as usual.

The next few weeks sped by and Louise got to know Ralph more and more. She went out with him on most evenings after her day at the gallery and, at weekends, they always arranged to do something, visiting other galleries, going to the cinema or the theatre and generally getting to know one another. Their feelings ran high for each other and they were content just being in one another's company. Louise could not imagine life without Ralph and openly declared her love for him, which was duly returned.

It was not long after their visit to the Albert Hall that they were at Ralph's studio. After a cosy evening together they were lying on Ralph's single bed. He was twisting her hair in his fingers and she in return was gazing into his eyes. He bent down and kissed her passionately, cupping her face in his hands. She spontaneously closed her arms around his waist, pulling his body closer to hers.

'I've wanted you for so long, Louise, but I don't want to pressure you if you are not ready.' Ralph could feel her melting in his arms.

'It's all right, darling. I want you too. I need you to show me how good it can be.'

With this, they slowly undressed each other and Ralph lovingly made love to her.

Peter Maze was always ready to direct a sarcastic remark at the young couple and he had become very remote towards Ralph. He still continued to ask Mary out and to question her about Louise and her intentions as regards to Ralph. Mary tried hard to keep the peace, but knew that Peter had more than a passing interest for her daughter. In fact she considered his feelings to be completely out of order and she became very protective towards Louise and Ralph.

One evening he had driven out to Mary's home and had actually declared his interest in her daughter and said that he could not understand what Louise could possibly see in Ralph when she could have him! This infuriated Mary and it took all her self-control not to tell Peter to leave her home there and then. How dare he be so arrogant as to think that her daughter would prefer him to Ralph? Also, she realised that Peter had been using her to get Louise and this was a feeling that she did not like at all. She also knew that Peter would spell trouble for them all as long as Louise worked for him at the gallery.

Later that same evening, when she was alone with Louise, she told her of her fears and of the conversation that she had had earlier with Peter.

Louise was horrified to think that her mother had been subjected to this behaviour by Peter and said she would hand in her notice at the end of the month. Mary said that she did not think that was a good idea as Louise so loved the work at the gallery and why should she leave because of the emotional pressure caused by Peter. Then Louise dropped the bombshell.

'Mother, I have got something that I must tell you: I am going to have a baby. I went to the doctor's this morning and he confirmed the test which I had done last week. I am eight weeks pregnant. I love Ralph, and I know that he loves me too. We are eventually going to get married and hopefully live happily together for the rest of our lives and so it does not really matter now what Peter Maze thinks or does because he will be wasting his time. I am sorry if this has come as an awful shock to you, but I just wanted to tell you when I was sure about the baby, and now I am certain.'

On receiving this news from Louise, Mary just burst into tears. This was the final straw. 'Everyone in my life has somehow let me down. I just feel as though I have been excluded from the secrets of the people I thought I was the closest to. I have thought of people to be who they are not and I have often been the last to know of what is really going on in the lives of my nearest and dearest.'

Louise stood back in horror at her mother's statement and realised that her mother was making reference to her late husband, Duncan. She had been dreading telling her mother about the baby, but tonight seemed the right time to break the news to her.

Mary regained her composure and said, 'I cannot say that I am pleased for you, Louise. If you were married, I would be really happy, but under the circumstances, your life will never be the same again and you will now have another human being to consider and he or she will need your undivided attention for the first few years of his or her life, and your concern for as long as you live. You assume that you will marry Ralph, but is he really prepared to take on a wife and a young baby at this stage in his life?'

Louise started to cry. 'I am sorry, Mother, I have not told him yet. I have not told anyone except for you and, of course, the doctor.'

Mary replied, 'Please don't cry, darling. I should think before I speak, but it has come as a great shock to me. I love you very much and I only want what is best for you. You really have a problem if you have not told Ralph. I just cannot imagine what his reaction will be. He is an artist and obviously relies on the sales of his paintings to live. Peter Maze told me the other night that he no longer requires Ralph's paintings at his gallery and so your guess is as good as mine as to where he will go to from there. My advice to you now is to telephone Ralph and invite him over and then the three of us can talk it all through.'

Without any delay, Louise went to the phone and called Ralph.

Chapter Nine

The next day dawned. Louise woke early with a very troubled mind. She knew the day had arrived when she had to tell the truth to Ralph. She got up with a slightly sick feeling, knowing perfectly well that this would be the first of many mornings for the next few weeks. She dressed herself in her jeans and a T-shirt and made some breakfast for herself and Mary.

Mary came down and asked how she was feeling about her forthcoming meeting with Ralph.

Louise replied, 'I will be all right Mother, but I am very nervous. Suddenly my confidence is waning and I keep imagining how Ralph will react to my news. I am wondering how well I ever knew him.'

'Keep calm, darling. I will back you up as much as I possibly can, but you must be prepared for his reaction. It presumably will come as quite a shock to him, although he must have known that this could result as the outcome of your actions!'

Breakfast was finished and cleared away. Louise and Mary eagerly awaited Ralph's arrival.

As soon as Louise saw him, her heartbeat increased. She loved him so much. He was her man and, if she lived until she was ninety, she would never have the feelings for another man as those she held for her young artist.

With his arrival, Mary said she would go and make the

three of them some coffee, tactfully leaving the two young people alone in the lounge to have a talk.

'Come and sit down, Ralph, as I have a great deal I would like to discuss with you.'

'All right, darling. I rather gathered from your telephone conversation that you needed to talk in person with me, so now that I am here, fire away.'

Louise took a deep breath and grabbed Ralph's hand. 'Ralph, there is no easy way to tell you this as I do not know what your reaction will be, but I am going to have your baby. It was confirmed by my doctor yesterday.'

A look of horror crossed over her lover's face. 'Oh, no, Louise! I am not ready for such a responsibility. You are just going to have to do something about it.'

Louise could not believe what she was hearing. 'But, Ralph, it will be our baby; we have created it together and nothing would persuade me to get rid of it. How could you possibly even suggest it?'

'Quite easily, Louise. At this moment in time I cannot and will not accept a baby into our lives. I am in no position to afford a wife, let alone a wife and a baby. I do love you in my way, but being an artist is a very precarious profession and already Peter Maze has told me that he has no further use for my paintings. I am truly sorry, Louise, but I also wanted to talk to you and tell you of my plans.'

At this stage, Louise really did not know what to say. She felt light-headed and a wave of nausea swept over her. She got up and ran to the bathroom and with her hands she steadied herself on the cool enamel of the washbasin. She turned the cold-water tap on and soaked her flannel, which she then held to her face. She continued to stand like that for a long time. She wanted to blot out all the words that Ralph had spoken so hastily and unkindly to her. She had not expected him to react in the way he had to the news of their baby and she was truly heartbroken.

After what seemed a long time, her mother came into the bathroom to see if she was all right. At the sight of her mother's anxious face, Louise broke down and cried her eyes out in Mary's arms.

'Come and sit down, Louise, and we will talk this situation through.'

Reluctantly, Louise put her flannel down and followed Mary into the lounge. Ralph was still sitting there as white as a sheet. He got up when they entered the lounge.

'I really am sorry about the baby, Louise. I wanted to ask you to come away with me to Paris, so that I could paint and hopefully sell my pictures there. We could make a fresh start and get right away from the likes of Peter Maze, who will do everything now in his power to prevent me from making a success of my career here in England. You must see the situation from my side of things, Louise. I love you but we would not be able to provide for a baby in a practical sense. We cannot live on dreams. You will have to be at home to care for the baby and I will be finding it more and more difficult to find galleries which will be willing to show my work, that is once Peter Maze has put the word around to his fellow gallery owners. I imagine he will make a good job of trying to destroy our future together. You know yourself how bitter he is.'

'No, Ralph, it is out of the question that I come to Paris with you, now or ever. My place is here and I shall continue to let our baby grow inside me and then love and care for it when the time comes. I suggest that you leave now and let me get on with my life and you must get on with yours.'

Ralph began to weep. 'I just cannot walk out of your life,

Louise. I love you and I want you to come with me to Paris. Please, darling, do not make a hasty decision.'

'My decision is made. Please leave now, Ralph. There is nothing left for the two of us to discuss.'

The nausea came back again and Louise felt her mother's loving arms go around her as she blacked out.

When Louise came round, she was lying on the sofa with pillows propping her head. It took her a little while to realise where she was, but as soon as she did, her memories of the recent events came flooding back to her and she looked across at her mother's anxious face.

'What a mess I am in, Mother; I just seem to have made mistake after mistake. I thought Ralph loved me and would be prepared to stand by me whatever, but I was totally wrong. I have been wrong about so many things lately.'

Louise slowly sat up and looked around. 'I gather that Ralph has gone?'

'Yes, darling,' replied Mary. 'He was very upset and felt he had caused enough harm to you. So I suggested, like you did, that he should go and I have told him that it would be for the best if he left for Paris as soon as it was possible for him to arrange. The cards are really stacked against him as well as you, darling. He is in no position to offer you and your baby a home and a future. I do feel he is being completely honest about that.'

'But if he really loved me, he would stand by me no matter what.'

'Louise, life is not as simple as that. Ralph is an artist; he is young and in love. He probably does not think or plan any further ahead than tomorrow. We will now just have to face the future and sort out your life and that of your baby. To me you are the most important person to consider and I shall look after you to the best of my ability.'

Louise felt her heart would break at her mother's words. She had been through so much sadness herself with losing her husband and discovering how betrayed by him she had been – but still she wanted to be there to give love and comfort. Yet who was there for Mary when she needed love and support? How cruel life was and now Louise was going to bring another human being into the world.

Mary asked, 'What are you going to do about your job at the gallery, Louise? I know you are not happy there and so maybe the time has come for you to leave and perhaps look for a part-time job in Putney or somewhere near to home. It would take the pressure off you having to travel backwards and forwards into town and soon the baby will begin to show!'

'Actually, I have been giving some serious thought to my job and I feel such resentment towards Peter Maze that I am going to leave. The baby has made up my mind for me and I shall be handing in my notice. I am obliged to give him a month's notice in writing and that will give him plenty of time to find a replacement for me. I think I shall be well rid of Peter Maze in my life and the same goes, I am sure, for you and also Ralph who, he is determined to try and ruin. Peter is a thoroughly unpleasant person and I, for one, will be thankful for never having to see him again.

Chapter Ten

A year passed and Louise had now become the very proud mother of a lovely son whom she had named Nicholas Ralph. Louise never would have believed what happiness this precious little person could bring into her life and to the life of her mother, Mary! Nicholas reminded her so much of Ralph. He had the same colouring and his little hands were like replicas of Ralph's. He was such a happy and contented baby with his large blue eyes and dark hair just as his father's colouring was.

After Louise had left the Maze Gallery, she had been lucky enough to obtain a part-time job in a small gallery in Wimbledon village. The owners had taken to Louise so much that they had said they would take her back when she was ready to work again after the baby was born.

This had made Louise very happy and Mary was quite prepared to look after her grandchild whilst Louise worked in the mornings at the gallery.

Although completely absorbed with taking care of Nicholas, never a day went by without Louise thinking and, at times, longing for Ralph, who was now installed in a studio flat in the poorer side of Paris. He had sent Louise his new address but his letter was very brief. She, in time, had sent him the news of Nicholas's arrival and so Ralph knew that he was a father. He again sent Louise a very brief letter saying how pleased he was for her, but never mentioned his reaction to receiving the news of their baby. He just added that he was keeping busy and was slowly selling some of his pictures and managing to scrape a modest living.

Now that Louise had her baby, her life settled down into a pattern. Nicholas wanted for nothing, and time and affection were given in abundance. It was only when she went to bed at night that her longing for Ralph sometimes became unbearable. It was not infatuation that she had felt for him; she really loved him and the hurt just would not go away. She thought that time would make it easier, but in her case it did not happen.

Louise did not feel a complete person without Ralph. He had awakened a longing in her and she needed him to make her feel whole. She imagined who he might be with now and whether he was committed to anyone. These thoughts would make her cry again and she worked very hard at controlling her feelings. Louise had learnt at a very young age, how terrible it was to want and to need someone and not be able to have them.

As the days slipped by, Mary continued to hope and pray that Louise would meet someone else for her to give her love to, but it was not to be. Poor Louise, she had lost Ralph and had had some of her time with him spoilt by the presence and sarcasm of a man such as Peter Maze. When Louise had left the gallery, she had told Peter that he was never to contact Mary or herself ever again and, when he had finally realised that she meant every word she said, he never did. They were certainly both well rid of that character.

Many a time Louise was tempted to ask Mary to look after Nicholas so that she could go to Paris and spend a little time with Ralph, but each time she had thought better of it. She could not be sure of her feelings if ever she was alone with him again. But she knew beyond a doubt that she would not need any persuading to be in his arms once again.

When Nicholas was six months old, Louise went back to the gallery at Wimbledon on a part-time basis and enjoyed meeting people, whether they were customers or artists, but it was good to go home at lunchtime to take over the caring of her baby.

One day, when Louise got home at lunchtime, her mother was looking very pale and anxious.

'Whatever has happened, Mother? You look as if you have seen a ghost. For goodness sake, will you tell me what is wrong?'

Mary replied, 'Please come and sit down, Louise. The post came after you had gone; a letter from Paris came addressed to me. It is from an artist friend of Ralph's informing me that Ralph is dead. They found his body in the Seine a week ago and he had left a letter for you with instructions for it to be given to you via me. This friend lived in the same house. You can imagine how I feel. I could not bring myself to phone you at the gallery, but it is my duty to give you the letter from Ralph.'

Louise took the letter from her mother with shaking hands and went into her bedroom to read it alone. The letter read:

My Dearest Louise,

By the time you receive this letter, I will no longer be in the land of the living. I have asked my good friend, Pierre, to forward this letter to you via your mother and I trust him to do as I have asked.

I have decided to end my life because I love you

and I have let you down. I should have stayed in England and become your husband and the father to our son. When you most needed me, I turned my back on you. I walked out of your life as though you had just been there for my convenience, to use you as I thought fit. All I thought about the coming baby was how it would make life difficult for me. I was not thinking of how it would affect you. I am an entirely useless and self-centred man.

I came to Paris, almost without a backward look, found this little studio and started to paint. Mostly pictures of the river – I spent hours and hours by the Seine. The one thing I did not reckon on though were my constant feelings I have for you, darling. Louise, in my utterly self-centred way, I love you, no, correction, I adore you. I feel that I have betrayed you and after all these months the feelings of guilt are becoming worse and I cannot live like this for much longer. I had thought of leaving Paris and coming back to England to be with you and our son, but that again is just not practical because, like before, I have nothing to offer you. Now the feeling I have utmost in my mind is to destroy myself – I am taking the only way out that I can come to terms with.

My dearest Louise – this letter is very difficult for me to write to you. Please be happy. I know that you will make a success of your life. I would have loved to have been the man who was always there for you, but as Mary once said to you, we artists are a different breed! You need a strong man as your partner in life and I hope one day you will meet that certain someone who will be there for you, to give you all the love and support that you so richly deserve.

> *When he is old enough to understand life, please tell Nicholas all about me and tell him about us – the good times we shared and how much I loved you, but that I was not the man for you. I know that you will give Nicholas all the love and support that I never could. I am taking the coward's way out, Louise, but I just cannot face the future.*
>
> *Ralph.*

Louise folded up her letter and put it into a drawer. She then went into the lounge to find Mary. Her life was now going to take on a new meaning – she understood what Mary had felt when she had lost Duncan, and she and her mother could forever share the love and be understanding of each other's loss of the men they had loved and then prematurely lost.

From the kitchen Louise heard the radio playing quietly the song called *Qué será será* – what will be, will be.

Part Three
Nicholas's Story

Chapter One

Nicholas woke, stretched and then opened his eyes very slowly.

It was the morning after his beloved grandmother's funeral. The bond that had grown between Mary and himself had been so very close. His grandmother had proved to be his grandparent, his friend and, above anything else, his mentor.

Nicholas had spent all his formative years living under Mary's roof and, in many ways, he always thought of himself as having two mothers, Mary and Louise. When his mother had married and consequently moved away to Sussex, Nicholas had chosen to remain with Mary and go on living in her home.

In many respects Louise had been saddened by Nicholas's decision and somewhat disappointed by her son's choice of his grandmother rather than herself, but Louise did understand that Nicholas's security lay mostly with Mary. She was also not blind to the bond which had developed between her mother and her son.

After several years, Louise had been introduced to a widowed brother of one of her old college friends and a mutual love and understanding had grown between them. When they had announced their intention of marrying, it had come as no big surprise to Mary, who was delighted for her daughter. Mary had always wanted Louise to find someone who would love and take care of her.

Louise was thirty-two when she married Robert and he had just had his fortieth birthday. Robert had lost his first wife. She had put up a very brave battle against breast cancer, but, after numerous operations and follow-up treatments, the cancer had won and she had died within eighteen months of the diagnosis. Losing his wife had left Robert alone and traumatised. His one consolation and his saving grace had been the very busy dental practice he ran in Barnes. His work, together with his patients' kindness, had kept him sane.

When Louise and Robert married, they had wanted, and both had needed, a fresh start in their lives and this had meant new surroundings and a new dental practice for Robert. They were very fortunate in finding their future lay in the little village of Meads on the fringe of Eastbourne in East Sussex.

'Good morning, Nicholas! I have brought you a cup of tea to wake you up.' Robert appeared in Nicholas's bedroom, complete with a cup and saucer in his hand. 'How did you sleep?'

'Fine, thanks,' replied Nicholas. 'Under the circumstances, I slept very well. I imagined that, after all of yesterday's proceedings, sleep would be difficult to achieve, but it was no problem and I feel better for the good night. How are you and Mum this morning?'

'Same as you; thankfully, we both slept well. We have decided not to rush back to Eastbourne though and I have already phoned through to one of my partners to cover for me for the next three days. This way we thought it would give your mother and me ample time to sort things out with you and decide what you are going to do.'

'That is great, Robert. I appreciate your and Mother's

concern and it is good to know that you will be around for a while longer.'

Mary had died peacefully in her sleep after a severe bout of bronchitis. She had been a heavy smoker and had taken to the habit ever since she had lost a baby daughter many years ago and had needed the comfort which a cigarette could give her. Despite constant warnings from her doctor, she could never bring herself to give up the weed and had continued to 'puff' away. She always maintained that smoking 'soothed her nerves! 'Well,' thought Nicholas, 'that was her excuse and she was sticking to it!'

Mary had made her eightieth birthday and so she did not think that smoking had caused her that much harm over the years! Also, having Nicholas to look after, she had never really been aware of growing old. Looking after him had given Mary a real purpose in life and she loved nothing more than having her home filled with his young friends. She never experienced the miseries that old age brought to her friends because she was too busy to have any time to brood on them!

Nicholas knew that, beyond a shadow of a doubt, he was really going to miss his grandmother. A wave of loneliness swept over him and he wondered how empty life was going to be at home without her. Mary had always been there for him and she had always wanted the best for him.

Robert appeared in his doorway again and broke his train of thought by saying, 'There are a few letters for you, Nicholas, and I thought you might like to read them in the privacy of your room.'

Nicholas realised that Robert was referring to the many kind letters of condolence he had been receiving since Mary's passing.

'Thank you, Robert, but I think I will go and have my

shower and get dressed before I open them. If you could just put them on my desk.'

His desk ran across the whole length of his window. When Nicholas had started to study as quite a young boy, Mary thought it best that he should work in his own room and so had arranged for a carpenter to built a unit, where he could house all his books and papers. Nicholas had spent many hours at his desk and still continued to do so; it had certainly provided him with the peace and quiet in which to work.

Chapter Two

After having completed showering and dressing, Nicholas sat on the end of his bed and opened up his mail. One of his letters was from the Westminster College and it contained some very good news! It was informing Nicholas that he had passed his final exams and had gained the highest grade possible in Hotel and Management. His instant happiness was quickly overshadowed by the fact that he was unable to tell Mary of his good fortune.

Nicholas had spent the last three years at the Westminster College studying hard and now all the hard work that he had put into the course had paid dividends. He thought how he would have loved to have had the chance to celebrate with Mary and for her to have been at the graduation ceremony. She would have loved it all, a chance to dress up and glow with pride as she watched her grandson collect his just rewards. However, it was not to be, but he quietly thanked Mary for all her love and help.

Nicholas left his bedroom in search of his mother and Robert. They were sitting opposite each other at the small, blue kitchen table and so he placed his letter between them to read and went over to the stove to pour himself a cup of coffee from the percolator.

'Well done, darling. Congratulations! I always knew you would do well and I really am very pleased for you. You deserve your success because you have worked so hard to achieve these excellent results.'

'Thank you, Mum; I only wish that Gran was here to share it all with us – I owe so very much to her.'

'I can imagine how you must be feeling, darling, but I am quite sure that she would want you to enjoy your success and she would be so very proud of you, just as Robert and I are.'

Mary had made such an enormous impact on both Louise's and Nicholas's lives and she was going to leave such a void for both of them. Louise thought back to the days when she had helped her through the darkest hours when she lost Ralph and had looked after her night and day when she gave birth to his son. Mary had been a mother in a million and life would never be the same for her or for Nicholas.

It had been Mary who had sat Nicholas down and told him all about his father and of his suicide in France. Somehow Louise could never find the strength to tell Nicholas about it herself and yet again, she had turned to her mother for help.

Nicholas had been fourteen years old when Mary had told him all about his father. She had told him very gently and she had watched his facial expressions very closely for his reactions. She need not have worried, as it turned out, as Nicholas accepted the facts very well and he only asked Mary a few questions, the main one being, 'If my father loved my mother so much, then how come he would not stand by her and marry her when he knew she was pregnant?'

Mary explained that at the time Ralph felt he could not afford to make that huge commitment and that, as an artist, he had not enough to offer. But Mary reassured him that he was a love child and there was no way that Louise would not have had him.

Nicholas looked at his grandmother and said, 'Thank you for telling me all about it, Gran. I might never have known my father, but it is certainly great to have two lovely ladies looking after me!'

From that time on, Nicholas just accepted life as it always had been for him and he never made any reference to that particular conversation which had passed between them. He was a very well-adjusted boy, who had done well at school and gone on to college to further his education.

When Nicholas first left school, he took a part-time bar job at a local pub on Putney Heath. He knew by then that he had been accepted by Westminster College to study for a degree in Travel and Tourism, but he enjoyed working in the bar and sometimes in the pub restaurant so much that he approached the college to see if he could study Hotel Management instead. This, fortunately, did not prove to be a problem and so he switched courses before having started! Nicholas was in no hurry whatsoever to leave home and he was more than happy to do a degree in London, rather than going away to university. Mary and he were so compatible and commuting to Westminster each day from Putney Bridge Station proved to be no hassle. He always looked forward to coming home at the end of a busy day to a good meal prepared for him by Mary. Afterwards he would take himself off to his room to study and to write his projects. Also, by now Nicholas felt very responsible for his grandmother and he liked being there for her. She had done everything in her power to provide a good and comfortable home for her grandson. Like his mother before him, he had had a very happy childhood, thanks to Mary.

Chapter Three

Now that the course was ended and Nicholas had obtained his degree, he had a great deal to celebrate. This was overshadowed by Mary's death, but Louise and Robert had made quite sure that a very happy evening was laid on for him to which they invited his closest friends. They started off by going to see the famous Agatha Christie play, *The Mousetrap*, which was followed by a marvellous dinner at The Ivy restaurant. The restaurant is nearly opposite the theatre and it proved to be a really good evening. All the right ingredients were there, a good play, good food and wine and good company; the only person missing was Mary. However, despite this, Nicholas had a wonderful evening of celebrations and to round off the evening he announced, 'I just want to let you know that I am now waiting for a reply to a letter that I have written to Trusthouse Forte applying for a job as an assistant manager!'

'Well done,' replied Robert. 'Well, our toast is: To Nicholas's future, and may you continue with every success in whatsoever you do.'

'To Nicholas's future,' they all replied and raised a glass of champagne to him.

Nicholas had decided to stay put after Mary's death. Mary had left her home in Putney to her grandson and so he decided to go on living there. Mary had also set up a trust for Nicholas and this would provide him with a monthly income, so his immediate living expenses, thanks to Mary's generosity, had been well provided for.

Louise had been left the bulk of Mary's estate, which would allow her to live very comfortably for the rest of her life. She certainly was not short of money and Robert provided them with a very substantial income from his practice. There were a good many elderly people living in the Eastbourne area and most were determined to retain their teeth, however much it cost them! Robert put up no argument to their wishes and worked extremely hard to provide them with what they needed. He and Louise lived in a very pretty Georgian house in Meads and the practice was run from an extension built to the left of their house. Robert had two partners, who worked full time with him, and they ran a thriving practice with the assistance of two very well-qualified dental nurses. Meads village was a typical Sussex village and the people who lived there really did seem to care about their neighbour's well-being. As it was a small community, their lives centred around their parish church of St John's, but when they needed a hospital or theatres and large hotels, they just took themselves off into Eastbourne. Meads village nestled at the foot of Beachy Head and sometimes, when Louise had the time, she would drive herself up there or sometimes in the summer she would walk up. On her arrival, she would spend a long time just watching the sea crashing on to the lighthouse and its surrounding rocks and she would be remembering Ralph.

Louise had so loved him. She loved Robert also, but in a completely different way from the way she had loved Ralph. Here, looking down at the sea, she thought back to her days at the Maze Gallery and all the fun, laughter and tears she had experienced in her time working there. Her thoughts were dominated by Ralph, and Louise still missed him and the love and closeness that one human being can share with another. After all the time that had passed, she still felt that physical yearning for him. But, apart from the memories, Ralph had given her their son. How fortunate she was to have Nicholas, who looked so like Ralph and who had inherited his loving ways. Louise felt such a deep love for Nicholas, who had given her a reason for going on after Ralph had gone from her life.

In the meantime, Nicholas had been granted his interview with Trusthouse Forte and, as a result, he had been offered the position as one of six Assistant Managers at the Cumberland Hotel. The General Manager of the hotel always had a team of six to assist him in the smooth running of the day-to-day life at the Cumberland. The hotel was one of the largest owned by Trusthouse Forte and it was situated in the very heart of London at Marble Arch. It was a very popular hotel with the overseas visitors, who found it very convenient for shopping, sightseeing and visiting the West End theatres and cinemas. In the hotel foyer there was always a constant stream of comings and goings. It housed its own shops, ticket agency and different restaurants and cafés. In fact, it was like a town on its own! There was even a taxi rank conveniently placed outside the entrance to the carvery bar.

Nicholas was exhilarated by it all and he felt a great need to give of his best at all times. He decided that he would commute to town each day from Putney Bridge Station, which just meant taking the District Line to Earl's Court and then catching the tube to Marble Arch. But the General Manager, Peter Baker, warned Nicholas that occasionally he would expect him to sleep in at the hotel during their peak times and also if Nicholas was working an evening shift.

Nicholas gained great satisfaction from his job and was more than pleased that it still gave him time for a social life. Like his mother before him, he had joined a tennis club in Kingston and spent many hours dashing about the courts! He made friends very easily and had gone to school in Wimbledon and so he had grown up surrounded by friends who lived locally.

Sometimes, if Nicholas had a free weekend, he would point his car in the direction of the A22 and spend a couple of days with his mother and Robert, who were always so pleased to see him.

On these trips down to see his mother, he wondered how often she thought about his father, but he came to the conclusion that she was perfectly happy and contented with her life with Robert. Robert was always very good to her and had seemed more than capable of proving to be a good husband for her. Nicholas liked and respected Robert and had always had a good rapport with his stepfather.

Chapter Four

After Nicholas had completed two extremely busy and rewarding years at the Cumberland, Peter Baker requested to see him in his office.

'Please come in, Nicholas, and sit yourself down. As you have most probably heard by now, Stephen Holden is retiring as our Conference and Banqueting Manager, and we would like to offer you the job. We are very pleased with the way you handle anything and everything to do with banquets, seminars and conferences. In fact, you have been extremely successful in all management matters whether it has been on the house side or whatever and we are more than confident that you could cope in this post!'

Nicholas did not hesitate for a moment. 'I would be delighted to accept the position and I regard it as a very great honour that you have asked me. It is rather strange, Peter, because, at some later stage, I was going to tell you that I am more inclined to the conference and banqueting side of management than I am to the general running of the house.'

'Well that is good news, Nicholas, and I am happy that you have accepted the position. We have realised over the last two years how you give of yourself one hundred per cent and how reliable you are. I wish you all the best as our future manager and many congratulations!'

When Nicholas returned home that evening, his first

port of call was the telephone. He had just poured himself a large gin and tonic and so, with a glass in one hand, he dialled his mother's number.

Louise's reaction to her son's news was instant. 'Nicholas, what wonderful news! Well done; I am so pleased for you, darling. What a responsibility for someone as young as you, but no doubt they feel that you are the right man for the job or else they would have advertised for someone else to fill the post. I am afraid that Robert is out playing squash this evening, but I will tell him your great news as soon as he returns home. I am pretty sure he will phone you with his congratulations! I know that you have been working at the Cumberland for just over two years now, but how do you find the travelling? Do you think it would be a good idea to get a flat up in town instead of travelling backwards and forwards to Putney?'

'No, Mum, I am fine and it all works very well for me and I really enjoy living in Putney – it is my base and it is quite a way from where I work – so please don't worry your pretty little head about me. I will not pretend to you that I am used to Gran not being here for me, she was quite a lady and I still miss her. However, over the past two years I have developed into a very contented bachelor!'

'Well, don't become too contented, darling. I would love to see you walk down the aisle one day!'

Mother and son continued to have a light and amusing conversation together and they both teased each other in a very light-hearted way.

'Is there any chance of you being able to come down to see us? It would be a great excuse to open the champagne and toast your success,' asked Louise.

'I am afraid not in the immediate future, Mum. I shall have to get myself organised in the new job before I can allow myself any time off!' replied Nicholas.

'Well, maybe Robert and I could come up to Putney and open up that champagne?'

'A great idea, Mum. You just let me know what you can arrange and we will take it from there!'

After putting the phone down, Nicholas poured himself another gin and tonic and settled himself down to read the *Evening Standard* to catch up with the goings-on in the outside world. It was a nice way to relax after a busy day.

When Nicholas finally got into bed that night, he lay there a long time thinking over the events of the day and planning how he could best approach his new job. He was really as pleased as punch at the prospect and could not wait to start on Monday! He considered it a very great honour that he had been asked to take this job on and he was determined to make a great success of it in every way possible.

Chapter Five

The months flew by and Nicholas was kept as busy as he had anticipated he would be. He had his own large office which was situated on the first floor of the hotel. It was dominated by a huge mahogany desk, at which a comfortable winged leather chair had been placed for Nicholas's use. The windows of the office overlooked Marble Arch and, beyond that, Hyde Park. He could not have asked for a lighter and nicer room in which to work. There were a couple of easy chairs set by a round coffee table, not to mention a cocktail cabinet which was always stocked with every conceivable drink! No, Nicholas had no complaints about his working environment at all!

His secretary, Joan, whom he shared with the Catering Manager, was in her mid-forties and had been in her job for over twenty years and there was precious little that she did not know about arrangements at the Cumberland. If in doubt – send for Joan! She was an excellent secretary and she tried to mother Nicholas at any given opportunity. She was forever checking that he had eaten or that a cup of coffee was there for him on his desk, complete with a couple of biscuits placed lovingly in his saucer. Joan meant well and Nicholas liked her for the warmth and concern that she always showed towards him.

Their first task each morning was to go through all the mail and check their appointments for the day. Nicholas then dictated the various replies and sometimes asked Joan to telephone people for him. They worked extremely well together and it had made it very easy for Nicholas to slot into his new job.

'You have an appointment at two o'clock today, Nicholas!' She had her diary open at today's date. 'It is a lady from a magazine and she said that she would like to arrange to hire one of our smaller conference rooms, which will hold up to forty people. She said that they will be requiring sherry and fruit juices on their arrival and then a buffet lunch to follow. Evidently, the purpose of the meeting is to hear how different magazines present their share of advertising. So I gathered that about four editors are hosting the lunch, with magazine staff who deal mainly with advertising.'

'For that number of people', replied Nicholas, 'it will have to be the 'Vanbrugh' room, Joan. Please will you check it out for me to see if it's free and then let me know before I meet the lady. Incidentally, do we have a name for the lady?'

Joan looked slightly ruffled. 'I am terribly sorry, but I have to confess that I do not know! She just said that she was telephoning us on behalf of *Vanity Magazine* and she never gave me a name and I have to say that I never asked her for one!'

'Not to worry, Joan. I will find out soon enough this afternoon when I get to meet her. In the meantime, I am going along to see Peter Baker to discuss the Christmas and New Year arrangements with him. So if you need me urgently in the office, just buzz me through.'

As the General Manager of the Cumberland, Peter always made sure that he spent some time every week with each of his managers. He was an excellent leader and always had his finger on the pulse! Very little happened at the hotel that he did not know about. Peter was well liked by his staff for his directness and fairness to them. He would let them know in no uncertain terms if something had been handled wrongly. But he never bore a grudge. He said what he needed to say and that was the end of it. But equally, he was the first to praise his managers if they deserved his commendation.

Peter got up from his chair when Nicholas was shown into his office by his secretary, Lynda.

'Come and sit yourself down, Nicholas,' Peter said warmly to his young manager. 'I really am very pleased at how well you are coping with your new position with us! I have heard nothing but praise from your team and often a guest has written in to me and said how efficiently you have set up a conference or a banquet for them. It's music to my ear. Well done!'

'Thank you, sir,' replied Nicholas. 'I appreciate what you have just said to me and I would like you to know that I enjoy the challenge that my new position gives to me and all the added responsibilities that it entails.'

After a little more time spent in general conversation, Peter asked Lynda if she would arrange for some sandwiches and coffee for them to have while they discussed the Christmas programme.

Christmas always had proved to be such a grand event at the Cumberland Hotel and a great many regular guests booked their places from year to year. In fact, the rooms were becoming harder to reserve unless you were a regular. More and more people wanted to come to the hotel and join in their Christmas festivities!

To Nicholas, Christmas seemed a long way off, but it was important for them to arrange the activities and meals very well in advance. This year, Nicholas would be adding some of his ideas to the season's events and would be helping guests to plan their festive occasions, whether it be 'Party Time', the 'Traditional Christmas Day Luncheon', the 'Boxing Day Buffet Bonanza' or the Cumberland's 'New Year's Eve Gala Ball'!

After a working lunch, Nicholas took leave of Peter and returned to his own office for his two o'clock appointment with the lady from *Vanity Magazine*.

He found a very smartly dressed young lady sitting on a chair by his office door, intently reading a newspaper. When Nicholas appeared, she looked up at him and he was immediately aware of her large blue eyes and her beautiful, shoulder-length, dark hair. She had a peaches and cream complexion and, to crown it all, she possessed the figure that a model would be proud of!

'Good afternoon, Mr Robson. I was told by your secretary to wait for you here!' Getting up from the chair, she held out her hand in greeting to Nicholas.

'Good afternoon to you,' smiled Nicholas. 'Please come into my office and sit yourself down. Can I offer you a cup of coffee or tea?'

'No, thank you; I have already had a drink in one of the bars and a round of sandwiches!'

When they had both sat down Nicholas said, 'I do apologise, but I am afraid that I don't know your name?'

'Please don't apologise, Mr Robson. I probably just said I was from *Vanity Magazine*, but by an enormous coincidence, I am called Miss Robson, Miss Sally Robson!'

Chapter Six

There was a stunned silence as they both studied each other with curiosity!

'How extraordinary,' Nicholas said, breaking the silence. 'I wonder if by any remote chance we have some family connection?'

'I really have no idea,' replied Sally. 'I certainly have never been told of a Nicholas Robson in our family!'

'Well seeing that I have another appointment at three o'clock. I wonder if I could be so bold as to invite you to have dinner with me one evening and then we can investigate the matter further.' Nicholas then added hurriedly, 'Of course, that is if you are not married or spoken for?'

Sally smiled. 'No, I am not married or, as you so old-fashionedly put it, I am not spoken for. I prefer to live the life of a career woman and that does not include allowing myself to make any heavy commitments to the opposite sex! Yes, in answer to your question, I would love to have dinner with you sometime.' Sally had not been slow in recognising a very handsome young man sitting opposite her!

'Great,' replied Nicholas. 'Now we can get down to business and sort out a room and requirements for your forthcoming meeting.'

The next hour was spent planning Sally's meeting and

by the end of the hour they had been able to arrange everything to both their satisfaction.

Nicholas got up and walked with Sally to the door of his office. 'It has been a real pleasure meeting you and doing business with you, Sally. I am more than a little intrigued with our shared surname and I shall look forward to our dinner date. Right, so we have agreed to make it for Tuesday, 9th May at eight o'clock. I suggest we meet here in the main bar of the hotel and have a drink, and then I will take you to a restaurant that I know of along the Chelsea Embankment – the food is excellent and I'm sure you will approve!'

'That sounds like a good idea and I shall look forward to the evening very much. So I will see you on the ninth at eight o'clock here. Thank you for arranging the magazine seminar for me. I will go back to my office and let everyone know the time and place for our day – I am quite sure it will prove to be a big success.'

Nicholas replied, 'Well, it is my job to make sure that everything will be done to make your day run smoothly. I would appreciate it if you could let me know as soon as possible which menu you will be requiring. Just give my secretary a call and we will then be able to confirm it all in writing for you.'

Once again, Sally gave Nicholas the benefit of her beautiful smile, which seemed to light up her whole face. 'Many thanks, Nicholas, for your efficiency; you have been really helpful. I will most certainly let you have the choice of menu in the next couple of days.'

Sally then shook Nicholas's hand and turned away in the direction of the Cumberland's side door where there was always a queue of taxis waiting to take their customers to their next destination.

'Wow,' thought Nicholas as Sally Robson went out of his view. 'That Sally is some lady!'

When Nicholas returned home that same evening, he telephoned his mother to ask her if she had ever heard of a Sally Robson. But he drew a blank when her answer was in the negative.

'Not to worry, Mum. I have arranged to take the lady in question out for dinner in a few days' time and I will have more time to talk to her. We really did not get much chance when she came to see me because we had to talk business for most of the time. It is probably just a coincidence, but I might add, an extremely attractive coincidence!'

Louise picked up immediately her son's interest in his afternoon business client! How often Louise had wished that Nicholas would meet that special someone; it would make her feel more content if she knew that he had a partner who would love and care for him. Nicholas had proved himself to be exceptionally independent and more than capable, but Louise felt that there must be times when he felt lonely since Mary's death. Also, Louise knew her son well enough to know that he would never admit how he felt to her, or for that matter, to anyone else. When Mary had been alive it was different because she had been such a great homemaker and she had seen to it that Nicholas would want for nothing.

After making his phone call to his mother, Nicholas went through to the kitchen and prepared himself a ham omelette and opened a bottle of wine. He poured himself a glass while he cooked and his thoughts returned to Sally. He felt excited at the prospect of meeting her again on the ninth. It had been a long time since he had been so taken with a young lady and hoped that the time would go quickly from now to their date together!

By the very nature of his job, Nicholas met a great many different people and some of them he took to straight away and some made little or no impression at all. But to say that Sally Robson had made an impression on him was an understatement! Even when Nicholas had cleared his supper away and settled himself down to watch some television, he still found his thoughts straying to his afternoon meeting with Sally. He wondered if she would investigate their surname with her family, or had she not given it another thought since leaving him?

Chapter Seven

Tuesday, 9th May certainly took its time in coming! The few days between Nicholas's meeting with Sally and the arranged dinner date seemed never-ending! But the evening eventually arrived and Nicholas showered and changed in one the hotel's bedrooms, which were laid aside for the members of staff as and when they needed them. Nicholas had driven up to town in the morning and parked his car in a multi-storey car park around the corner in Mount Street. He always preferred to travel by car when he was spending the evening in London.

At a quarter to eight he headed for the main bar in the foyer. The head barman, Tim, was on duty and he came over and asked Nicholas what he would like to drink?

'It's fine, thanks, Tim. I am meeting a guest here at eight o'clock and then I'll order for the two of us. We are having a drink here and then going for dinner at the Dolphin Restaurant, which as you well know, is one of my favourite haunts!'

'Ah! The Cumberland not good enough for you?' joked Tim.

'Well, under the present circumstances, no!' replied Nicholas. 'I will have all the staff talking and there will be no way I would be able to relax!' Nicholas knew only too well that he had only to be seen off duty with a pretty woman at his side and the news spread!

The two men continued chatting together and then at precisely eight o'clock, Sally walked into the bar. She looked really stunning in a midnight blue dress with a matching jacket. The blue of her dress made her eyes seem bluer than ever,

Sally walked over to Nicholas with her hand outstretched. 'Hello, Nicholas; it's good to see you again!'

Nicholas shook her hand warmly and felt really happy to see her. 'Hello, Sally. You look really lovely.' Nicholas was well aware of the many admiring glances that had followed Sally across the bar! 'Would you like a champagne cocktail or a different drink?'

'That would be fine. I am very partial to champagne!'

They sat themselves down at one of the many little tables in the bar and Tim brought them their champagne cocktails. Nicholas could see the approving look which he gave to Sally and felt obliged to introduce them! Sally chatted easily to them both and there was certainly no question of not feeling relaxed in Sally's company – she positively radiated warmth.

'I have booked our table for nine o'clock at the Dolphin Restaurant and so when you are ready we will drive over there.'

'Ready when you are, Nicholas!' replied Sally.

So with a final approving look from Tim and a cheery 'good night' they set off for their dinner date.

Nicholas was well known at the Dolphin Restaurant as he had used it many times during the last couple of years. In fact, he had spent his twenty-first there when Louise and Robert had generously hosted a party for thirty of his closest friends. It had certainly been an evening for him to remember and a very good time had been enjoyed by all present.

'Good evening, Mr Robson. It is good to see you again.' The Restaurant Manager was genuinely pleased to see Nicholas. 'I have reserved a table for you overlooking the river as you requested.'

The manager led them over to a table which, as well as having a view of the river, had the added advantage of being in full view of the band and the postage-stamp-sized dance floor.

After Nicholas and Sally had settled themselves down at their table, Sally said, 'It really is an attractive setting, Nicholas. I have driven past here quite a few times and often thought that I would like to go inside, but I have always been *en route* somewhere and never got round to it. It certainly is very smart, but it has a happy atmosphere to it, which I picked up as soon as we arrived. Yes, I am really going to enjoy myself this evening!'

'Well, that's good to hear!' replied Nicholas. 'I have always been more than pleased with the evenings I have spent here and with the service. It is also great to find a restaurant where you can wine and dine and be able to have a dance. The band usually starts playing at around half past nine.'

The conversation flowed easily between the two young people and Nicholas felt as though they had always known each other.

'Now,' began Nicholas, 'have you been able to find out anything further about our mutual surname? I telephoned my mother, but she certainly had never heard of a Sally Robson!'

'Well, I have to confess that I also have been unable to find out any more because my mother is away in Canada for three months at present visiting some cousins. She has gone with her brother and my father died before I was born.'

'We seem to have drawn a blank then,' replied Nicholas. Sally smiled. 'Not to worry, I shall make a point of asking my mother on her return to England. It is probably a sheer coincidence that we share the same surname, but it is certainly worth a little further investigating!'

Once their meal had reached the dessert stage, Nicholas told the waiter to leave a little gap before they ordered and then invited Sally to join him on the dance floor. The band was now in full swing and several other of the diners had ventured on to the floor. The band was playing a quickstep to a very catchy little tune and Nicholas and Sally found themselves dancing naturally in rhythm to the music. Nicholas held Sally very close to him and he liked the feel of her body in contact with his. It all felt very good.

When they had danced for quite a long time, they returned to their table and ordered their desserts. Sally told Nicholas all about the training she had done in journalism and how, for the past seven years, she had worked for *Vanity Magazine* at their offices in Regent Street.

'I hope you do not mind me asking you, Sally, but how old are you? If you trained for three years and you have already been with your magazine for seven years – where have you reached?'

'I have just turned thirty-two,' replied Sally without the slightest hesitation.

'Well, that's fantastic!' exclaimed Nicholas. 'You really do not look a day over twenty-two, never mind being thirty-two!'

'Thank you, kind sir. You must know that flattery will get you everywhere!' laughed Sally. 'Well, it is your turn now. How old are you?'

'I have to confess that I am your junior! I am coming up

to twenty-four.'

'You certainly look very mature for only twenty-three,' said Sally. 'I would have put you somewhere around the twenty-eight mark.'

Their talk during the evening was all very light-hearted and happy. They both enjoyed a really good time spent in each other's company. They stayed at the restaurant until just after one o'clock enjoying the music and their coffees and going back on to the dance floor several more times. At the end of the evening, Nicholas drove Sally to her home in Knightsbridge.

'Many years ago my mother worked as a secretary at the Maze Gallery in Knightsbridge which is quite close to where you live. Do you know the gallery?' asked Nicholas.

'I certainly do,' replied Sally. 'But the original owner, Peter Maze died about seven years ago and left it to a nephew of his, a John Turner. I hear that he runs the gallery very well. I haven't visited it recently, but it is on my list of places to go, that is if I can find the time!'

Nicholas smiled to himself as he knew only too well what it was like not to have enough hours in the day in which to do all you would like to! He decided at this point not to mention to Sally that his father had exhibited some of his paintings at the gallery.

Nicholas brought his car to a standstill outside Sally's home, but she did not invite him in. It was late and they both had their work in the morning. Nicholas got out of his car and went round to the passenger's side to open the door for Sally. He accompanied her to her front door and gave her a kiss on each cheek and promised to call her again very soon.

'Thanks for a wonderful evening, Nicholas; it was magic! I thoroughly enjoyed myself and I have the song out of the show *My Fair Lady* going around in my head. "I could have danced all night", and I really could have, if only work was not on my immediate horizon!'

Nicholas drove home on cloud number seven! He had so enjoyed being with Sally and was already thinking about the next time he could see her.

Chapter Eight

Nicholas was extremely busy during the summer months and it proved to be a real bonus if he could get away for any length of time to visit his mother and Robert. However, it was now July and his birthday was looming up towards the end of the month. This invariably meant that his mother would want to see him and, at the best, want him to spend a few days with her!

Just as Nicholas had thought, his mother phoned him one evening with his expected invitation!

'Darling, do try to come down to us for the weekend of your birthday – you know that we would love to celebrate with you.'

'I have been working on the weekend rota today, Mother, and I have made sure that my birthday weekend is covered by one of my very capable assistants and so I will be with you and Robert! I have given myself an extra day and so I will be arriving on the Friday.'

'That's really good news, darling. Robert and I will be looking forward to seeing you. The last few months we do not seem to have had very much contact, but we do know how busy the hotel gets with so many foreign visitors in London in the summer months.'

'Yes, it has been hectic, to say the least! But I have a great team working for me and they are one hundred per cent reliable, so what more can I ask?'

'Well, it goes without saying how very proud Robert and I are of you, Nicholas.'

'By the way, Mother, would it be all right with you if I brought my friend, Sally, to stay for the weekend? Incidentally, Sally is the young lady who shares the same surname as me!'

'Of course it will be all right, darling. It will be nice to meet her – it's not often that you ask me if you can bring a friend with you and she will be most welcome.'

'Thank you, Mum; I appreciate it.'

'After I have finished talking to you, I will telephone to book somewhere for dinner on the Saturday night. Do you have somewhere in mind where we can go?'

Nicholas replied, 'I favour the Hydro Hotel; the food is excellent and the service is efficient. Also you do get a little background music there on a Saturday night, even if it is a bit old-fashioned!'

'A good choice, Nicholas. It also is near enough for us to be able to walk there and get some sea air. Robert and I sometimes go into Eastbourne for a meal, but it always means going by car. It is good to have somewhere really nice to eat which is in walking distance!'

'Right, that is settled then. Sally and I will be arriving sometime on the Friday and we will look forward to seeing you then.'

After replacing the receiver, Nicholas thought how very comfortable his relationship was with his mother and how she must have been torn apart when she had married Robert and left him to live with his grandmother. When you are young, you do take your mother for granted and never think about what is affecting her and all the emotions she has to endure – the young are very selfish! Despite not having lived with his mother on a permanent basis, he felt very secure in her love for him.

Since the evening at the Dolphin Restaurant, Nicholas had taken Sally out for dinner on several occasions and had always enjoyed being with her. She made him feel good and, above all, she had a great sense of humour! It was certainly a 'first' to have asked his mother if he could bring a young lady to stay for the weekend!

Sally had been very pleased when Nicholas had invited her to spend his birthday weekend at his mother and stepfather's home and she was looking forward to it and to meeting his parents.

Vanity Magazine had held their seminar at the Cumberland Hotel and Nicholas had arranged everything for them to perfection. Several of the ladies were very impressed with Nicholas's efficiency and had already expressed their desire to return to the Cumberland for any further seminars or functions. Nicholas was becoming used to praise, but it did not alter his down-to-earth approach to his job and his above-average communication with his clients and guests. He was just grateful that he was doing his job well and that all his efforts and hard work were being appreciated.

Nicholas drove Sally down to the coast on the Friday afternoon of his birthday weekend. It was a beautiful summer's day, with blue skies and sunshine all the way.

'Because the weather is so perfect, Sally, I think we will take a drive up to Beachy Head and enjoy the views before going to Mother's. Is that all right with you?'

'A good idea, Nicholas. We can enjoy the views and have a walk and breathe in some sea air after all the fumes we get in London!'

They arrived at Beachy Head at about three o'clock and the cliffs were bathed in glorious sunshine. Nicholas parked his car in a public car park where there was a roadside café and so they decided to have a cup of tea first before their walk.

After they had had their tea and reached Beachy Head, Nicholas was more than surprised to see his mother standing near the edge and looking at the sea! She was oblivious to anyone or anything around her and so Nicholas approached her very gently, so as not to frighten her. He walked up to her, put his arms around her and gave her a hug.

'Oh, Nicholas, what a surprise! What are you doing up here? I thought you would be going straight home. Robert has taken the afternoon off and is waiting for you!'

'We are doing the same as you, Mother – enjoying the spectacular views on this beautiful day! Most important, Mum, please meet Sally!'

Louise gasped as she looked at the lovely girl whom Nicholas had just introduced to her. She so reminded her of someone she had met so many years ago. Louise quickly gained control and held her hand out to Sally.

'Welcome to Eastbourne, Sally. I have heard a lot about you and it's a pleasure to finally get to meet you!'

'It is quite reciprocal, Louise. I have been looking forward to meeting you and thank you for having me to stay for the weekend,' replied Sally with a warm smile.

'So what are you doing up here, Mother?' asked Nicholas. 'I imagined you would be at home awaiting our arrival! Sally and I only decided to visit Beachy Head on the spur of the moment so we could see all the views in this gorgeous weather.'

'I really came up here for exactly the same reason as you two did,' replied Louise.

Louise decided not to add that she had come up here because it was here that she felt closest to Ralph. As this was the weekend of their son's birthday, she needed to spend some time alone with her memories. She could still, after all these years that had passed, feel Ralph's love and lust for her and she still felt the overpowering longing for him, which time had failed to heal.

Sally walked a little nearer to the edge and looked over to the lighthouse below, with the sea crashing over the rocks which surrounded it. It was strange that, on a beautiful calm day such as today, the sea around the lighthouse was still threatening and wild, whereas the rest of the sea was as calm as a millpond.

Sally said, 'This view is exactly like a painting in my Uncle David's home. My mother purchased it for him a long time ago, knowing how much her brother loved pictures of the sea. It was painted by a very young, talented artist by the name of Ralph Waters, whom my mother did have the pleasure of meeting very briefly, when she was at the gallery buying the picture.'

Nicholas could not believe what he had just heard and his first reaction was concern for his mother. Louise's colour had drained from her face, as she remembered Sally's mother, Anne Robson, coming into the Maze Gallery and writing out a cheque for the painting of Beachy Head for her brother.

Turning to Sally and quickly trying to compose herself, Louise said, 'Ralph Waters is Nicholas's father and many years ago I worked in the Maze Gallery and I sold the painting to your mother, Anne.'

Now it was Sally's turn to listen with disbelief at Louise's words. 'Well, how amazing! So you actually got to meet my mother all those years ago!'

Thoughts were spinning around in Nicholas's head and he asked his mother, 'Is it just a coincidence that Sally and I have the same surname or is there a definite link?'

Chapter Nine

Louise felt that, under the circumstances, it would be more appropriate to continue their discussion back at her house. So they abandoned the idea of a walk and decided to drive back to Louise's home in Meads village.

After Sally had been introduced to Robert and shown around the house, Louise poured them all a drink, which she took out into her lovely Sussex garden. The garden furniture was colourful and comfortable and the four of them sat themselves down, armed with a drink and somewhat apprehensive about the conversation to come! It was a really perfect summer's day and they had so much to talk about.

Nicholas was the first to speak. 'Come on, Mother, it really is up to you to explain what is happening and to satisfy our curiosity – there is probably so much you can tell us. I think that, given the chance, we would all prefer to know the truth and then we can speak about the past with openness.'

Nicholas could see Louise physically taking in a few deep breaths before saying, 'When you telephoned me a few weeks ago to ask me if I knew of a Sally Robson who had any connection with our family, I genuinely could think of no one whom I knew with that name. As I have always been somewhat reluctant to rake up the past, it certainly did not stir up any memories. I just accepted your question at face value and replied to you accordingly. However, when I saw Sally up at Beachy Head with you, then something certainly sparked off my memory. Am I right in saying that you are the image of your mother, Anne?' Louise was looking straight at Sally, when she asked her this question, a question asked with a mixture of directness and honesty.

'You are perfectly correct, Louise. All my life people have been quick to tell me how very much like my mother I am. In fact, I will even go so far as to say that I can see it clearly for myself! We have the same colouring in our skin and our features are identical – two peas in a pod!' replied Sally, who answered Louise's question with the directness it deserved.

Sally had taken instantly to Louise and had quickly sensed that she was a sensitive woman and now it appeared she had had a troubled past. A wave of sympathy went out to her. Poor Louise had certainly not bargained on this meeting through her son.

Louise continued, 'I think also, Sally, I would be right in saying that your father was killed in a car accident before you were even born?'

Sally replied, 'Yes, as a matter of fact he was. In fact, he was killed on the very day that my mother was going to tell him that she was pregnant with me and so my poor mother had a double shock – not only had she lost my father, but she never had the joy of telling him about me.'

The two men, Robert and Nicholas, were listening with great interest and growing concern for Louise and Sally, but were sitting silently and neither felt like interrupting.

A short silence was broken by Sally's next question.

'It is incredible that you know these facts about me, so was it my mother who told you all about it all those years ago?'

'No,' replied Louise. 'Your mother did not need to tell me. The reason I know is because your father also happens to be my father!'

Sally stared at Louise. 'But this is incredible! I knew that my mother and father were not married because he was already married to someone else. My mother has told me very little about him, except that his name was Duncan Robson and she was very much in love with him, as he was with her.'

At this point, Sally broke down and started to cry. It was all becoming a bit too emotional for her and the shock of this conversation was upsetting her. Nicholas got out of his chair and went over to put a protective arm around her and offered her some much needed comfort.

'What a dreadful situation we have all ended up in. I ask you down to my mother's home to celebrate my birthday and it has stirred up a hornet's nest. I will go and get us all another drink – we certainly need something to relax us.'

Nicholas came back into the garden with a fresh drink for each of them and then sat back in his chair to listen to what was to come next. Sally took a little while to compose herself. Louise looked at her forlorn face and was full of compassion for her. She was such a lovely young woman and she looked so vulnerable sitting there, listening to a stranger telling her that they shared the same father.

How strange, thought Louise, that she was destined to know about her father's past. Her concern also was growing for her son, Nicholas. She knew that he had strong feelings towards Sally and that, after all that had been revealed, there was no way that their relationship could go any further forward. Sally was Louise's half sister and, technically, it made Sally Nicholas's aunt.

'You know, Louise,' Sally said, 'I have always felt that

there was a big gap in my life not having a father and I always used to envy my friends at school and at college when they talked about their fathers and I met them. They had something that I had always wanted in my life. In fact, I felt cheated that I didn't have one. Now, at last, if it is not too painful for you, could you tell me about him? I think that it will help me to accept this situation that has transpired.'

Louise did not hesitate for one minute with her reply.

'Of course I will be happy to talk about him to you, Sally, but I was only beginning to get to know him myself when he was so abruptly and cruelly taken away from us. But I do have some very happy memories of him and I am just terribly sorry that you never had the chance to know him. He was quite a striking personality and you certainly could never be in a room at the same time as him and not know he was there!'

'My mother has always been very guarded about how much she tells me about him. I think she feels a sense of guilt that he belonged to someone else and somehow she finds it difficult to talk about him in front of me. My guess is that if ever she needs to talk about her life with him, then she does so with Uncle David. It was Uncle David who first introduced them and so he was very much part of the relationship which developed. Mother has always been close to her brother and I am sure there have been many times when she's cried on his shoulder. I have proved to be a constant reminder of her great love for my father and, at times, I feel desperately sorry for her. I know it was wrong to be so in love with a married man, but none of us ever know who we are going to meet and how different relationships will turn out.'

'How very true; we meet people, get involved with them

and often there is no going back. Love is a very strong emotion and it will send the most sensible person into complete turmoil. When I was a great deal younger, I often used to listen to a record sung by Doris Day, called *Qué será será*, which translated means 'What will be, will be' and I am a firm believer in that, Sally. Even in my darkest moments, when I lost Nicholas's father, these words kept returning to my mind and in some strange way, they give me comfort and hope for the future.'

All four of them talked well into the night. There was just so very much to talk about. Louise had prepared a salmon salad with Jersey new potatoes, which they ate in the garden. This was accompanied by two bottles of Louise's favourite white wine, Niersteiner – a wine which she could tell Sally their father was a great lover of!

When Nicholas was alone in the kitchen helping Louise with the clearing up he said, 'Well, Mum, talk about dropping a bombshell! I could hardly believe what I was hearing! It has been like one enormous jigsaw puzzle, with all the pieces slotting into place. It is odd, but however close I have felt towards Sally at times, something has held me back from expressing my true feelings for her. Do not begin to ask me why, but I have always felt that something was not quite right about our relationship. It was absolutely nothing to do with the fact that she is ten years my senior. In fact, to be perfectly honest, I cannot pinpoint this feeling that I have always had when I am with her. I want you to know that it is not 'the end of the world' because all this information has come to light and I certainly do not want you to worry yourself, because I can assure you now that there is nothing for you to worry about. I am perfectly happy with my life as it is and I am sure that one day a certain young lady whom I will want to be with all the time will come into my life, but I can honestly say that that certain someone I am yet to meet! At the time of going to press, I have a wonderful mum, a super stepfather, a terrific job and a host of good friends to enjoy my life with and also I have discovered a glamorous 'auntie' to add to it all – what more could a fella need?'

'Oh darling, thank you for saying all that. I cannot begin to tell you what you mean to me and how very much I love you. A very happy birthday!'